瑞蘭國際

瑞蘭國際

搭配詞的力量
THE POWER OF COLLOCATIONS

形容詞篇

序

對於很多台灣的大學畢業生而言,畢業後「不務正業」做一些和主修八竿子打不著的工作已成為一個普遍的現象。而我能將我的大學、研究所所學,緊緊地和我的工作——英語教學——緊扣著,用著這樣的「幸運」好好做些什麼事,是我一直感激的。

2011 年 9 月,受到 Pit Corder 一篇 1967 年的經典文章〈The Significance of Learner Errors〉當中所述,對於了解「怎麼學」要在了解「怎麼教」之前之必要性所啟發,我毅然決然從賓州大學離開至哥倫比亞大學教育生研究院,在那開啟了對於第二語言習得(Second language acquisition)的深度學習。

在學習過程中,影響我特別深的,是一位叫韓照紅(ZhaoHong Han)的中國籍女教授。認識她的人,包括很多學界的教授,都知道她講話鏗鏘有力,授課風格極為嚴格且犀利。讓對知識有真熱情的學生,修習她的課程如入寶山。

對於精通中文、英文、日文,也曾經粗淺地學習過法文的我,她曾經跟我談到,因為我有眾多學習語言的經驗,我會有更多更準確的「直覺」(stronger intuitions),知道可能什麼才是較正確的學習語言方法,而我們可以再去用實證研究去驗證那些直覺。也就是在研究第二語言習得的過程當中,認知到了「chunking-based learning」(語塊學習)的重要性。

眾多認知心理學研究顯示,我們的大腦,相對於「離散」(discrete)的資訊,對於記憶一塊有連結性、有系統的資訊群比

較在行。而「collocations」（搭配詞）的學習，即是因應大腦這樣的特性。同時也可以讓我們在思考字和字如何搭配使用時，防堵我們的「中文想法」或「中文概念」滲透進去。搭配詞就是一個詞組，而這個詞組裡頭可能包含兩個甚至兩個以上習慣搭配在一起的字（A collocation is a familiar grouping of words, especially words that habitually appear together.）。由於每個語言都有它們習慣組合字詞的方式，所以熟稔搭配詞對於幫助我們正確且道地地使用語言，會有極大的幫助。

例如，我們中文可以說「學習新知」，但是「learn new knowledge」卻是錯誤的英文。例如，當我們要表達「確切的日期」時，英語母語人士能夠直覺地、不假思索地使用出來「a firm date」，這也是搭配詞的力量。更不用說英文母語人士公式般地（所以也有人稱搭配詞為 formulaic expression），使用出「gain a deeper understanding of sth」（對於～有更深入地了解），這也是搭配詞所互相結合的產物。

但相對於學習者，英語母語人士在習得搭配詞的過程是一個較自然、不費力的過程，甚至有可能不自覺。但對於第二外語學習者來說（成人尤是），由於先天後天條件和學習環境都較不利，需要有一個管道，能接觸到眾多的搭配詞。

因為這樣的一個契機，我從 2015 年起辦了超過 100 場搭配詞學習免費公開課，也在 2016 年創建了「搭配詞的力量」Facebook 專頁。在出版品上，在 2017 年發行了《搭配詞的力量

Collocations：名詞篇》一書。本書《搭配詞的力量 Collocations：形容詞篇》，如同名詞篇般，結集了眾知名搭配詞字典（Macmillan Collocations Dictionary, Oxford Collocations Dictionary, BBI Combinatory Dictionary of English, Longman Collocations Dictionary and Thesaurus）和種種語料庫，整理出台灣人最需要的搭配詞、以及沒有記憶的話極容易受到「中文腦」影響而用錯的搭配詞。目前市面上的搭配詞用書，大多是厚重的字典，沒有中文翻譯輔助，有時也過度繁雜，比較像是工具書，其實不太適合學習者直接學習。除此之外，我也特別鼓勵讀者在使用本書時，善加利用本書的附帶光碟一起學習，讓學習時能夠利用「聽覺的語言輸入」（audio input）提升學習效果。

　　《搭配詞的力量》一系列書，希望站在巨人的肩膀上，能夠提供對搭配詞學習有興趣的台灣學習者，最直接的幫助。希望本書能作為學習者一個新的立基點，從今以後能讓「語塊學習」、「搭配詞」等等的新觀點，有效提升英語能力，不再「字字是英文，句句非英文」，「年年學英文，年年從頭學」。

創勝文教共同創辦人

王梓沅

06/26/2018

搭配詞如何能給你力量？
為何搭配詞那麼重要呢？

★ 你是否有想要講一句話，但是語塞講不出來，因為「不知道要用什麼字表達心中所想的東西」的經驗呢？

★ 你是否有時會覺得自己的英文看似「字字是英文」，但其實「句句不是英文」，不知如何道地、精準地使用英文呢？

★ 你是否知道的單字不少，但是真的用出來的總是那些呢？

　　如果你曾經有以上的感覺過，那麼很可能代表你的英文搭配詞記得不夠多喔！英語母語人士之所以講話能如此精準、流利，其中一個原因來自於他們頭腦中有眾多的搭配詞，幫助他們有效率、精準地表達想法。若我們用中文習慣的方式去思考字與字的組合，就很容易造成很多的「台式英文」（Chinglish）。其實很多的搭配習慣，是沒有什麼原因的（arbitrary）。我們直接來看看以下幾個英語搭配詞。

　　對中文母語人士來說，我們會不假思索地講出「吃藥」。但對英語母語人士而言，「eat medicine」卻是個錯誤的表達方式（英文：take medicine）。而你知道嗎？在日文裡頭，他們的藥是用喝的喔（日文：薬を飲む）！

　　這樣的差異，其實在語言中，屢見不鮮。

　　例如，我們再來看看中文、英文在祝賀人生日時的差異。

　　於中文母語人士來說，「生日快樂」是我們會不假思索使用的。但你有注意到嗎？對我們的「中文耳」而言，「Happy Birthday」

（生日開心）這樣的賀詞，是較不通順的。但當 Happy 這個字，「開心」跟「快樂」都是合理的翻譯時，我們的「中文腦」要如何去做選擇呢？而日本人卻是用「生日恭喜」（お誕生日おめでとう）呢！

《搭配詞的力量 Collocations：形容詞篇》一書，即因應台灣人學習英語的需求而生。作者從語料庫中整理出英語學習者頻繁使用的形容詞，並列出和其搭配使用的名詞以及慣用法等，並精選例句輔以學習，希望能夠加深大家對這些高頻形容詞的認識。

例如，就「bitter」這個字而言，不少人知道是「苦」的意思。但在「bitter」一章節當中，本書就介紹了「bitter dispute」這樣的用法，也就是「激烈的爭執」的意思喔！而像在「empty」一章節中，介紹了像是「empty promise」（空頭支票）如此的用法，讓我們對於「empty」的認識，從知道是「空」，到能夠進一步知道如何使用這個字。

一個語言要學好，一定要用對方法。希望這本書所載錄的搭配詞，能帶給大家在學習上，滿滿的力量。Happy learning!

範例：bitter

Bitter 苦的；痛苦的；激烈的；尖酸的；嚴寒刺骨的
▶ MP3-008

bitter blow 沉重的打擊

The news came as a bitter blow to the staff.
這消息對員工來說是個沉重的打擊。

bitter disappointment 極度的失望

The trite ending to this film is a bitter disappointment.
這部電影老套的結局讓人非常失望。

bitter experience / lesson 慘痛的經驗 / 教訓

She learned through bitter experience that he was not to be trusted.
她從慘痛的經驗中學到：他不可信。

bitter fruit 苦果

The unemployed are tasting the bitter fruits of the market economy.
失業的人正在享受市場經濟的苦果。

bitter memory 痛苦的回憶

The photo stirred up her bitter memories.
這張照片勾起她痛苦的回憶。

bitter argument / controversy / dispute / quarrel
激烈的爭論、爭執

There was a particularly bitter dispute over payment for working overtime.
加班費問題引發非常激烈的爭議。

bitter battle / conflict / fight / struggle
激烈的衝突、苦戰

The couple is locked in a bitter battle for the custody of the children.
這對夫妻陷入爭奪孩子監護權的苦戰。

bitter disagreement / opposition 強烈的分歧 / 反對

The government faced bitter opposition to these policies.
政府面臨對這些政策的強烈反對。

bitter enemy / rival 勁敵、死對頭

The two men are bitter rivals for the party leadership.
這兩人是爭奪黨主席大位的對手。

bitter feud / hatred 強烈的仇恨

The two men were members of a gang involved in a bitter feud between rival families.
這兩人是幫派的成員，而幫派則捲入了敵對幫派間的仇恨。

A
B
C
D
E
F
G
H
I
J
K
L
M
N
O
P
Q
R
S
T
U

28

29

創勝文教共同創辦人

王梓沅

2017 年 3 月

目次

C　　　　　　　　　　　　　　　　　　　　　　043

Chronic	慢性的、長期的；慣常的
Clear	清澈的；清楚的、（思維）清晰的；明顯的、無疑的；免除的；不接觸的；完整的；空閒的
Compelling	強而有說服力的、有趣的、強烈的
Competitive	競爭力強的、有競爭力的、激烈的
Comprehensive	全面的、綜合的、詳盡的
Concerted	共同的、協力一致的
Considerable	相當大的、相當多的

D　　　　　　　　　　　　　　　　　　　　　　061

Decent	正派的、得體的、相當好的
Deep	深的；（程度）深的、極度的
Deep-rooted	根深蒂固的
Difficult	困難的、艱難的；難相處的
Downright	完全的、徹底的
Drastic	劇烈的；嚴厲的

E　　　　　　　　　　　　　　　　　　　　　　073

| Easy | 容易的；舒適的、自在的、放心的 |
| Effective | 有效的、（法律、制度）生效的 |

Empty	空的、無人的；空虛的、空洞的、無意義的
Exhaustive	全面的、徹底的、詳盡的
Exorbitant	（價格、要求）過高的、過分的、離譜的

Fair	公正的、公平的；合理的；相當大的；晴朗的
Fast	快速的；放蕩的；牢固的
Fat	肥胖的；厚的；（利潤、費用）豐厚的；極少的
Favorable	稱讚的、正面的；有利的、適合的
Fertile	肥沃的、富饒的、能生育的、點子多的
Fine	好的、傑出的；（身體狀況）良好的；細微的、精確的、精緻的
Firm	穩固的；確定、確切的；嚴格、強硬的；堅定、堅決的
Flat	平坦的、扁平的；（容器）淺的；（飲料）沒氣的；（輪胎、球）洩氣的；（電池）沒電的；緊貼的；平淡的、缺乏熱情的；斷然的、肯定的；（金額）固定不變的；（市場、交易）蕭條的、不理想的；恰好的
Fresh	新的；無經驗的；無禮的、輕佻放肆的；精力充沛的

Genuine	真正的；真誠的、真心的

Hard	困難的、艱難的；堅硬的；努力的、勤奮的；用力的；嚴格的、冷酷無情的；嚴寒的；確實的、不容懷疑的；烈的
Harsh	嚴厲的；惡劣的、艱苦的；刺眼的、刺耳的
Hasty	匆忙的；倉促的、草率的
Heartfelt	衷心的、真誠的
Hearty	衷心的、熱情的；大量的、豐盛的；盡情的；健壯的
Heated	激烈的、憤怒的
Heavy	重的、厚重的；繁重的、費力的；劇烈的、大量的；（心情）沉重的；（食物）難消化的；（情況）嚴重的、麻煩的
Hectic	忙碌的、繁忙的
Hidden	隱藏的
High	高的；（地位、程度）高的、重要的；情緒高昂的、正盛的；含量高的

Inclement	（天氣）惡劣的、嚴酷的
Instant	立即的；緊急的、迫切的
Intense	強烈的、劇烈的、熱烈的

Keen   熱切的、渴望的；強烈的、激烈的；敏銳的、銳利的

Large   大的；大量的；大規模的

Lenient   仁慈的、寬厚的

Liberal   開明的；自由的、開放的；慷慨的、大方的；大量的；
                        模糊的、籠統的

Light   輕的；明亮的、淺色的；少量的、輕微的；輕鬆的、輕
                        快的

Loose   寬鬆的、鬆動的；不受控制的；零散的；不嚴謹的、大
                        略的

Low   低的、矮的；（地位、程度）低的、卑微的；消沉的、
                        低落的；含量低的

Major   主要的、重大的；大部分的；主修的

Massive   巨大的；大量的、巨額的；大規模的；（病情）嚴重的

Minor   次要的、不重要的、不嚴重的；小部分的；副修的；未
                        成年的

Moderate   中等的、適度的、有節制的；溫和的、不偏激的

P 181

Pathological	不受控制的、病態的、非理性的；疾病的
Perennial	長期的、不斷發生的
Poisonous	有毒的、有害的；令人極不愉快的、惡意的
Prolific	多產的、作品豐富的
Promising	有希望的、有前途的
Prompt	即時的、迅速的

Q 190

Quick	快速的、立即的；聰敏的

R 193

Rapid	快速的、迅速的
Rash	草率的、魯莽的
Relentless	持續的
Rigorous	嚴格的、嚴謹的
Robust	健壯的、健全的；強勁的、堅定的、果決的；濃郁的、濃烈的
Rough	粗糙的、崎嶇的；粗略的；艱難的、難受的；粗製的、未加工的；粗暴的、粗俗的；（天氣）惡劣的

Sensitive	敏感的；易受影響的；機密的；靈敏的
Serious	重要的；嚴重的；嚴肅的、認真的；大量的、過多的
Shaky	搖晃的、顫抖的；不穩定的、不可靠的
Sharp	尖的；劇烈的；明顯的；敏銳的、精明的；尖酸刻薄的
Significant	重要的、值得注意的；大量的、顯著的
Slight	小的、細微的
Slim	苗條的；少許的
Smooth	光滑的；平穩的；流暢的、順利的；圓滑的；（酒、咖啡）順口的
Soft	軟的、柔滑的；溫和的、軟弱的；柔和的、輕聲的；（市場、貨幣）疲弱的、不穩定的；輕鬆的
Solid	堅硬的、結實的、實心的；確定的、可信賴的；不間斷的、持續的；一致的
Sound	健康的、完好的；合理的、可靠的；穩固的；熟睡的
Stable	穩定的、平穩的；可靠的、穩重的
Stark	嚴酷的；明顯的、極度的
Steep	陡峭的；急劇的；（價格）過高的
Stiff	硬的、挺的；僵硬的、不自然的；強烈的、激烈的；嚴厲的、艱難的；（價格、代價）高昂的
Straight	直的、正的；坦誠的、直率的；嚴肅的；僅涉及兩者的；整齊的；連續不間斷的；互不欠錢的
Striking	顯著的、驚人的、出眾的、引人注目的

Strong	強壯的；堅定的；強烈的；有力的；穩固的、（關係）緊密的；很有可能的；（味道、氣味）濃的；擅長的
Superficial	外表的、表面上的；粗淺的、草率的；膚淺的
Swift	快速的、立即的

T 262

Tall	高的；誇大的
Tentative	暫定的、試驗性的、試探性的
Thin	瘦的；細的、薄的；稀少的、稀薄的；空泛的、微弱的
Tight	嚴格的；緊的、緊密的；勢均力敵的
Tough	（肉）過熟的、咬不動的；難對付的、強硬的；堅強的、堅定的；艱難的
Toxic	有毒的；令人極不愉快的、惡毒的、造成陰影的

V 277

Vague	模糊的、不清楚的
Vigorous	激烈的、強烈的；有力的、積極的；旺盛的、茁壯的

W 281

Weak	弱的；無力的；無能的、沒影響力的；疲軟的、蕭條的；稀的、淡的
Wide	寬的；很大的；廣泛的
Widespread	普遍的、廣泛的

Abrupt 唐突的、突然的、陡峭的

▶ MP3-001

abrupt question 唐突的問題

The speaker was irritated by the abrupt question raised by the reporter.
這位講者被記者所問的唐突問題惹怒。

abrupt slope 陡坡

He did not dare to bike down the abrupt slope.
他不敢騎腳踏車下這個陡坡。

abrupt change 突然的改變

A volatile environment differs from a stable environment in that changes in the former tend to be profound and abrupt.
易變環境和穩定環境主要的差異在於，在易變環境中的改變常常都是巨大且突然的。

abrupt end 驟然的結束

Sandy's peaceful life came to an abrupt end after her parents' marriage fell apart.
珊蒂的安穩生活在她父母離異後驟然結束。

Acid 酸的、尖酸刻薄的、決定性的、嚴峻的

▶ MP3-002

acid flavor 帶有酸味的

My mom likes apples with a slightly <u>acid flavor</u>.
我媽媽喜歡略帶酸味的蘋果。

acid test 決定性的、嚴峻的考驗

This match will be the <u>acid test</u> to see if the team is truly strong and competitive.
要看這支球隊到底是否真的強而有競爭力，這場比賽可見真章。

acid remarks 尖酸刻薄的發言

Her <u>acid remarks</u> got on the nerves of many of her opponents.
她尖酸刻薄的發言惹怒了很多她的對手。

Acute
急性的、劇烈的；極度的、非常嚴重的；
敏銳的

acute condition / disease / illness / infection
急性的疾病

This term indicates an <u>acute disease</u> of such severity that immediate surgical intervention must be considered.
這術語表示這是嚴重的急性疾病，必須考慮立即進行手術。

acute pain 劇痛

Suffering from <u>acute</u> abdominal <u>pain</u>, she was taken to the hospital.
她因為劇烈腹痛被送往醫院。

acute anxiety / concern / distress / embarrassment
極為焦慮 / 擔心 / 痛苦 / 尷尬

The report has caused <u>acute embarrassment</u> to the government.
這份報告使政府極為難堪。

acute crisis 嚴重的危機

The war has aggravated an <u>acute</u> economic <u>crisis</u>.
戰爭使嚴重的經濟危機更加惡化。

acute problem 嚴重的問題

Poverty is a particularly <u>acute problem</u> in this area.
貧窮是這個地區相當嚴重的問題。

acute shortage 嚴重的短缺

There are <u>acute shortages</u> of food and medical equipment in some countries.
有些國家的糧食和醫療設備嚴重短缺。

acute awareness 敏銳的意識

Politicians now have much <u>acuter awareness</u> of these problems.
政客現在對這些問題有更敏銳的認識。

acute insight 敏銳的洞察力、眼光

He has <u>acute insight</u>, which makes many people feel admired.
他有敏銳的眼光，讓許多人都很佩服。

acute intelligence 機敏聰穎

She is a British writer of <u>acute intelligence</u>.
她是個機敏聰穎的英國作家。

acute sense of sth 敏銳的～感

We firmly believe that dogs have a particularly <u>acute sense of</u> smell.

我們深信狗有特別敏銳的嗅覺。

Adverse 不利的、有害的、負面的 ▶ MP3-004

adverse effect / impact 不利的、負面的影響

They are afraid that the incident could have an <u>adverse effect</u> on global financial markets.
他們擔心這個事件會對全球金融市場造成不利的影響。

adverse conditions 不利的條件、情況

The event was cancelled because of <u>adverse</u> weather <u>conditions</u>.
由於天氣惡劣，活動被取消了。

Arduous 費力的、艱苦的、曲折的 ▶ MP3-005

arduous work 辛苦的工作

The work will be arduous, but it will give you a great sense of achievement.
雖然這將是份十分艱苦的工作，但它會給你很大的成就感。

arduous task 艱苦的任務

Finding that special someone can be an arduous and lengthy task.
找到那個特別的人是一項巨大且漫長的任務。

arduous process 辛苦的過程

Learning a foreign language can be a long and arduous process.
學習外語是個漫長又辛苦的過程。

arduous path 曲折的道路

The path to truth can be an arduous one.
通往真相的路常常是崎嶇的。

Big
大的；重要的、嚴重的；影響大的、程度大的（用於強調）；年紀大的；宏大的；成功的、有名的

big day 重要的日子、大日子

All of the family members are ready for the <u>big day</u>.
全部的家族成員都已經準備好迎接這個重要的日子。

big word 艱深難懂的字

He tried to impress his professor by using <u>big words</u> in all his essays.
他試著在所有的文章中用艱深的字，讓教授留下好印象。

big drinker 酒量很好、很能喝

He always claims that he is a <u>big drinker</u>, but that is not the case.
他老說自己酒量很好，但其實不然。

big eater 食量很大、很能吃

He used to be a <u>big eater</u>, but somehow he has little appetite recently.
他以前很能吃，但不知怎麼最近卻沒什麼胃口。

big increase / decrease 大幅增長、減少（也可以説

significant increase / decrease）

The big decrease in revenue was mainly attributed to
aggressive advertising by rival dating sites.
本公司營收大幅減少的主因為敵對交友網站猛烈的廣告攻勢。

big picture 一件事的全貌；最重要的目標

In my political work, I try to concentrate on the big picture
and not be distracted by details.
在政治工作上，我試著著眼全局，不為枝微末節分心。

big spender 揮霍無度的人

Don't be a big spender because money doesn't grow on
trees.
不要揮霍無度，錢不是從天上掉下來的。

big brother / sister 哥哥 / 姊姊（= older brother / sister）

＊ Big Brother 字首大寫時也有「監視人民行為的獨裁政府」之意，此用法源自於
  英國作家 George Orwell 的作品《1984》

Paul is my big brother, studying Social Economics at LSE.
保羅是我哥，他在倫敦政經學院攻讀社會經濟學。

big idea 偉大的理想、抱負、想法

Jasper has had big ideas about starting up his own
company.
賈斯伯的抱負是創辦自己的公司。

big name 大人物、名人

I'm sure all the <u>big names</u> will attend tonight's award ceremony.
我確定所有名人都會出席今晚的頒獎典禮。

實用短語 / 用法 / 句型　　▶ MP3-007

1. **to be big of sb** 某人真好心、真慷慨（反諷用法）
   It <u>was big of</u> you to admit that these problems are really your fault.
   你真好心啊！承認這些問題都是你的錯。

2. **to be big on sth** 很喜歡某事物
   She <u>is big on</u> language. She really likes learning about the differences between languages.
   她對語言很有興趣，喜歡研究語言的差異。

3. **to be big / great with child** 懷孕多時，通常是指快要生小孩了
   My wife, who <u>is big with child</u>, is on her way to the hospital.
   我大腹便便的老婆正在去醫院的路上。

4. **to be / get too big for one's boots** 自以為是、自大
   She has been <u>getting too big for her boots</u> since she got that promotion.
   她自從那次升遷後就變得越來越自大了。

5. to give sb a big hand 為～鼓掌、給予～掌聲

Ladies and gentlemen, let's give a big hand to our special guests.

各位來賓，讓我們以熱烈的掌聲歡迎特別來賓。

6. to have a big mouth

大嘴巴，形容一個人愛說閒話、守不住祕密

I'm not going to tell him the secret as he has a big mouth.

我不會告訴他這個祕密，因為他是大嘴巴。

7. to make it big 成功、出名、做大

We're not just looking at making it big in Taiwan. We want to be big internationally.

我們不只是想在台灣成功，更要享譽國際。

8. to talk big 吹噓、說大話

We don't like those who talk big and do nothing.

我們不喜歡只會說大話卻不做事的人。

9. to think big 眼光放遠、放大格局

If we want to succeed, we need to think big.

如果想成功，我們就該把眼光放遠點。

10. to use / wield a big stick

採取強硬手段，例如運用權力施壓來獲取想要的事物，此用法源自於美國老羅斯福總統的巨棒外交政策

The trade unions were afraid that the government would wield a big stick over them.

工會擔心政府會對他們採取強硬手段。

11. great big 非常大的（口語用法）

There is a <u>great big</u> storm approaching the town.
We should evacuate all the civilians right now!
強烈風暴正逼近這個小鎮，我們必須立即撤離所有居
民！

12. in a big way 大規模地、程度上很大

She always likes to do things <u>in a big way</u>.
她老是喜歡把事情搞得轟轟烈烈。

13. no big deal 不要緊、沒什麼

We'll have to pay a little more, but it's <u>no big deal</u>.
我們不得不多付一點錢，但這不要緊。

Bitter 苦的；痛苦的；激烈的；尖酸的；嚴寒刺骨的

▶ MP3-008

bitter blow 沉重的打擊

The news came as a bitter blow to our staff.
這消息對員工來說是個沉重的打擊。

bitter disappointment 極度的失望

The trite ending to this film is a bitter disappointment.
這部電影老套的結局讓人非常失望。

bitter experience / lesson 慘痛的經驗 / 教訓

She learned through bitter experience that he was not to be trusted.
她從慘痛的經驗中學到：他不可信。

bitter fruit 苦果

The unemployed are tasting the bitter fruits of the market economy.
失業的人正在承受市場經濟的苦果。

bitter memory 痛苦的回憶

The photo stirred up her bitter memories.
這張照片喚起她痛苦的回憶。

bitter argument / controversy / dispute / quarrel

激烈的爭論、爭執

There was a particularly <u>bitter dispute</u> over payment for working overtime.

加班費問題引發非常激烈的爭論。

bitter battle / conflict / fight / struggle

激烈的衝突、苦戰

The couple is locked in a <u>bitter battle</u> for the custody of the children.

這對夫妻陷入爭奪孩子監護權的苦戰。

bitter disagreement / opposition 強烈的分歧 / 反對

The government faced <u>bitter opposition</u> to these policies.

政府面臨對這些政策的強烈反對。

bitter enemy / rival 勁敵、死對頭

The two men are <u>bitter rivals</u> for the party leadership.

這兩人是爭奪黨主席大位的對手。

bitter feud / hatred 強烈的仇恨

The two men were members of a gang involved in a <u>bitter feud</u> between rival families.

這兩人是幫派的成員，而幫派則捲入了敵對幫派間的宿怨。

bitter rivalry 激烈的競爭

There is a <u>bitter rivalry</u> between the two countries.
這兩個國家間的激烈競爭。

bitter irony 尖酸諷刺

We were struck by the <u>bitter irony</u> of the situation.
這情況的酸言酸語大大震驚了我們。

bitter wind 刺骨的寒風

Outside, a <u>bitter</u> east <u>wind</u> is accompanied by flurries of snow.
外面寒冷的東風刺骨，還伴著陣陣小雪。

實用短語 / 用法 / 句型　　▶ MP3-009

1. **to the bitter end** 堅持到底、拼到底
   Many climbers gave up before they reached the summit, but we were determined to stick it out <u>to the bitter end</u>.
   很多登山客在成功攻頂之前就放棄了，但我們決心要撐到最後。

2. **a bitter pill (to swallow)** 必須接受的殘酷事實
   Losing to a beginner was <u>a bitter pill to swallow</u>.
   輸給初學者是個難以接受的殘酷事實。

Blunt 鈍的、不鋒利的；直率的

▶ MP3-010

blunt instrument 鈍器

The victim suffered a blow to the head from a <u>blunt instrument</u>.
受害者的頭部遭受鈍器重擊。

blunt statement 直率的表達、聲明

His <u>blunt statement</u> that he'd resigned concealed his anxiety about the situation.
他直言不諱地表示自己已經辭職，這隱藏了他對情勢的擔憂。

實用短語 / 用法 / 句型

▶ MP3-011

1. **to be blunt** 坦白說
   <u>To be</u> perfectly <u>blunt</u>, the last piece of work you did was terrible.
   坦白說，你的最後一件作品爛透了。

Boundless 無限的

▶ MP3-012

boundless energy / enthusiasm 無限的精力 / 熱情

He never fails to impress us with his genuine interest, in-depth knowledge, and <u>boundless energy</u>.

他的熱誠、淵博的知識及無限的能量一直使我們印象深刻。

boundless imagination 無限的想像力

As a highly prolific novelist, J.K. Rowling is known for her <u>boundless imagination</u>.

身為多產的小說家，J.K. 羅琳以她無限的想像力聞名。

boundless possibility

無限的可能（也可以說 endless possibility）

Many companies recruit interns because of their great curiosity and <u>boundless possibilities</u>.

許多公司招募實習生，因為他們擁有強大的好奇心和無限的可能。

Brief 短暫的；簡短的、簡潔的

brief appearance 短暫的露面、亮相

She made a <u>brief appearance</u> before the reporters outside the conference hall.
她在會議廳外的記者前短暫露面。

brief encounter 短暫的碰面、相遇

I did not see her again, except for a <u>brief encounter</u> on a train.
除了在火車上短暫的相遇，我再也沒見過她。

brief interlude / period / spell / stint 短暫的時間

After a <u>brief spell</u> in the army, he started working as a teacher.
在部隊待了一段時間後，他就開始從事教職。

brief look / glance / glimpse 匆匆一瞥、快速瀏覽

Before we go into details, let's take a <u>brief look</u> at the basic structure of the proposal.
在進到細節前，我們先看一下這個提案的基本架構。

brief moment 短暫的片刻

The professor's gaze rested on the sleeping student for a <u>brief moment</u>.
教授的眼神在睡著的學生身上停留了一下。

brief stay / visit 短暫的拜訪

Hugh Jackman made a <u>brief visit</u> to Taiwan last month.
休傑克曼上個月短暫拜訪台灣。

brief stop 短暫的停留

We will soon make a <u>brief stop</u> at Banqiao station.
本列車即將抵達板橋站。

brief account / description / sketch 簡短的描述

Please give a <u>brief description</u> of the photo on this page.
請簡短描述一下這頁的照片。

brief chat / talk 簡短的談話

She stopped me this morning at the office and we had a
<u>brief chat</u>.
今天早上她在辦公室把我叫住，我們稍微聊了幾句。

brief discussion / explanation 簡短的討論 / 解釋

After a <u>brief discussion</u>, they decided to accept the offer.
經過簡短討論，他們決定接受這個提議。

brief introduction / outline / overview / summary / synopsis 簡介、概要

I will provide you with a <u>brief summary</u> of this article.
我會提供你們這篇文章的摘要。

brief mention 簡短的提及

Later I will make a <u>brief mention</u> of the theories we explored last week.
稍後我會簡短提到我們上個禮拜探討的理論。

brief note 簡短的便條、備註、筆記

I would like to add a <u>brief note</u> on that issue on behalf of my team.
我想代表我的團隊針對那個議題做簡短補充。

brief statement 簡短的聲明

The spokesman made a <u>brief statement</u> to the press, dispelling the doubt surrounding the company.
發言人向媒體做了簡短的聲明,消除外界對公司的質疑。

實用短語 / 用法 / 句型　　▶ MP3-014

1. **in brief** 簡言之、總而言之
   <u>In brief</u>, the President plans to cut defense spending, lower taxes, and welcome the immigrants.
   總之,總統打算削減國防費用、降低稅賦、接受外來移民。

2. 「**brief** +一段時間」 指一段短暫的時間
   For a few <u>brief minutes</u>, we forgot the anxiety and anguish.
   才幾分鐘,我們已經忘了剛剛的焦慮和痛苦。

Bright 明亮的、鮮豔的;樂觀的、有活力的、有希望的;聰明的

▶ MP3-015

bright lights 都市的繁華生活、誘惑

In 2008 I moved to New York, attracted by the <u>bright lights</u> of the city.
因為深受紐約繁華的都市生活所吸引,2008 年我搬去了那裡。

bright future / outlook / prospects 光明的前景

According to its stock performance and annual report, it seems that the company has <u>bright prospects</u> ahead.
根據該公司的股票表現和年報,公司的前景似乎一片光明。

bright spot
亮點(特別是在其他事物都表現不好時,成功或值得高興的事)

The smartphone industry is the <u>bright spot</u> in the economy at the moment.
智慧型手機產業是目前經濟的亮點。

bright idea 聰明的想法、好主意

She is constantly coming up with <u>bright ideas</u> for making money.
她不斷想到一些賺錢的好主意。

1. to look on the bright side 往好處想、抱持樂觀態度

Look on the bright side—things can only get better from now on.

往好處想，從現在開始，事情只會變得更好。

2. (as) bright as a button 聰明伶俐的（英）

He is bright as a button—always asking good questions.

他聰明伶俐，總是提出些很好的問題。

3. bright and breezy 樂觀有自信的

He may seem bright and breezy now, but he often felt melancholy when alone.

他現在看起來可能很樂觀有自信，但他一個人的時候常常感到憂鬱。

4. bright and early 大清早

We have to get up bright and early in the morning to catch the flight.

我們必須一大早起床趕飛機。

5. bright spark

看似聰明卻做蠢事的人、蠢蛋（反諷用法）

Some bright spark left the key in the door.

哪個人這麼聰明把鑰匙留在門上。

Brisk 輕快的;興隆的;簡潔幹練的

▶ MP3-017

brisk pace 輕快的步伐

Penny set off at a <u>brisk pace</u> for the movie theater.
佩妮踩著輕快的步伐前往電影院。

brisk walk 快步走、輕快的散步

Taking a <u>brisk walk</u> is good for your health.
快走有益健康。

brisk business / trade 生意興隆

Vendors at amusement parks do a <u>brisk trade</u> in souvenirs.
遊樂園裡紀念品攤販的生意很好。

brisk tone / voice 簡潔幹練的語調

She answered the phone in a <u>brisk voice</u>.
她用簡潔幹練的語調講電話。

Broad

寬的、遼闊的；廣泛的；概括的、粗略的；明顯的

▶ MP3-018

broad grin / smile 露齒笑

Tina showed up with a <u>broad smile</u> on her face.
蒂娜面帶笑容出現。

broad agreement / consensus 廣泛的共識

The world leaders finally reached <u>broad agreement</u> on climate change.
各國領袖終於就氣候變遷達成廣泛的共識。

broad appeal 廣泛的吸引力

The Beatles' music had a very <u>broad appeal</u> at that time.
披頭四的歌曲在當時有相當大的吸引力。

broad range / spectrum 廣大的範圍

High school students in Taiwan are required to study a <u>broad range</u> of subjects.
台灣高中生必須學習的科目範圍很廣。

broad support 廣泛的支持

The government has gained <u>broad support</u> from the public.
政府贏得民眾廣泛的支持。

broad framework / outline 大致的框架、輪廓

We are supposed to provide a broad outline of our plan today.
我們今天必須給出計畫的大綱。

broad overview 概述

In the first week, the professor will give students a broad overview of what microeconomics is.
教授會在第一週概述什麼是個體經濟學。

broad hint 明顯的暗示

I received a broad hint that they did not want me to call again.
我收到明顯的暗示：他們不希望我再去拜訪。

1. broad-based 範圍廣泛的、影響廣泛的

The current economic slowdown will be broad-based, affecting all regions of the US.
目前經濟衰退的影響廣泛，波及全美國。

2. in broad daylight 光天化日之下

It is reported that the thieves broke into the house in broad daylight.
據報導，竊賊在光天化日之下闖入房子。

3. in broad terms 廣泛來說、一般而言

The client should understand, in broad terms, the likely cost of the case.
一般而言，客戶應該要了解案件可能需要的成本。

4. in the broadest sense of the term / word
從最廣義的解釋來看、廣義來說

This film is successful, in the broadest sense of the word.
廣義來說，這部電影是成功的。

Bumpy 崎嶇不平的、顛簸的

bumpy landing 顛簸著陸

The plane made a <u>bumpy landing</u> because of bad weather conditions.
由於天氣狀況不佳，飛機著陸時顛簸不穩。

bumpy ride 顛簸、艱困的過程

Shares had a <u>bumpy ride</u> yesterday, falling by an average of 15%.
昨天股市走勢顛簸，平均下跌了 15%。

bumpy road 崎嶇不平的道路

People in the area have gotten tired of the rocky and <u>bumpy road</u>.
這地區的居民已經受夠了那條崎嶇不平的路。

Chronic 慢性的、長期的；慣常的 ▶ MP3-021

chronic anxiety / depression / fatigue / stress
長期的焦慮 / 憂鬱 / 疲倦 / 壓力

Sometimes <u>chronic fatigue</u> can be a sign of more serious problems.
有時候長期感到疲倦可能是更嚴重問題的徵兆。

chronic condition / disease / disorder / illness / infection 慢性的疾病

The drug is widely used to treat all types of <u>chronic diseases</u>.
這種藥被廣泛用來治療各種慢性疾病。

chronic lack / shortage 長期的短缺

There is a <u>chronic shortage</u> of teachers in remote areas.
偏鄉地區長期缺乏教師。

chronic need 長期的需要

There is a <u>chronic need</u> to address poor turnout.
長期以來我們都需要解決低投票率的問題。

chronic poverty 長期的貧窮

One cause of the man's suicide seems to be chronic poverty.
長期貧窮似乎是這個人自殺的原因之一。

chronic problem 長期的問題

Air pollution has been a chronic problem in Beijing.
空氣污染已經是北京長期的問題。

chronic unemployment 長期的失業

Chronic unemployment has led to chronic alcohol and substance abuse problems.
長期失業導致了長期酗酒和吸毒的問題。

chronic alcoholic / complainer / worrier
酗酒的人 / 常抱怨的人 / 常煩惱的人

The sleep patterns of chronic alcoholics are usually quite abnormal.
酗酒的人睡眠模式通常很不正常。

Clear 清澈的；清楚的、（思維）清晰的；明顯的、無疑的；免除的；不接觸的；完整的；空閒的

▶ MP3-022

clear conscience 無愧

Let them say whatever they like. I have a <u>clear conscience</u>.
他們想怎麼說就怎麼說，我問心無愧。

clear head 清醒的頭腦

I won't have another drink. I need to have a <u>clear head</u> for my meeting in the morning.
我不喝了，我早上要開會，必須保持頭腦清醒。

clear idea / picture / understanding 清楚了解

We should have a <u>clear picture</u> of the situation and what opportunities are available to us now.
我們必須搞清楚狀況，還要了解現在有什麼可行的機會。

clear look / view 清楚看見、清楚的視野

From the top floor, we can get a <u>clear view</u> of the Eiffel Tower.
我們能從頂樓清楚看見艾菲爾鐵塔。

clear case / example 明顯的例子

His statement was a <u>clear example</u> of racial discrimination.
他的說法很明顯有種族歧視。

clear distinction 明顯的差別

There's no <u>clear distinction</u> between the dialects spoken in the two regions.
這兩地區的方言沒有明顯的差別。

clear majority 明顯的多數

The ruling party has won a <u>clear majority</u> in parliamentary elections.
執政黨在國會選舉中拿下過半席次。

clear victory 明顯的勝利

Her party won a <u>clear victory</u> in the elections.
她的政黨在選舉中大獲全勝。

實用短語 / 用法 / 句型　　▶ MP3-023

1. **to be clear of sth** 免除、擺脫某事物
   After a two-hour interrogation, he <u>is</u> now <u>clear of</u> all suspicion.
   經過兩小時的訊問，他現在已經排除所有嫌疑了。

2. **to be in the clear**
   沒有嫌疑的；脫離險境的、沒有危險的
   The government investigated the charges against the company and decided it <u>was in the clear</u>.
   政府對該公司的指控進行調查，並認定它沒有嫌疑。

After staying in the intensive care unit for a few days, he is now in the clear.

在加護病房待了幾天，他現在已經脫離險境。

3. **to get / make sth clear** 弄清楚、解釋清楚某事

Many people have difficulty in making their feelings clear when it comes to love.

談到愛情時，很多人都很難清楚表達自己的感受。

4. **to see one's way (clear) to doing sth**

同意、允許

We expect good results soon, if the board can see its way clear to continuing funding the project.

如果董事會能同意繼續資助這個計畫，我們預期很快就會有好結果。

5. **to stay / steer clear of sth**

與某物保持距離、避免接觸某事

Please stay clear of the closing doors.

關門時請勿強行進出。

His speech steered clear of controversial issues.

他的演說避開了爭議性議題。

6. **(as) clear as a bell** （聲音）清晰洪亮的

Clear as a bell, from the playground came a child's voice.

遊樂場傳來一個小孩清脆洪亮的聲音。

7. **(as) clear as day** 顯而易見的；容易理解的

I wish these legal contracts were <u>as clear as day</u> so that there would be no confusion.

我真希望這些法律合約能清楚好懂一些，這樣就不會有任何疑問。

8. **(as) clear as mud** 不清楚的、難理解的（反諷用法）

His instructions were <u>as clear as mud</u>—I have no idea how to get there.

他的指示一點都不清楚，我完全不知道該怎麼走。

9. **crystal clear** 非常清楚、極其明白的；非常清澈的

The boss is <u>crystal clear</u> about what he wants to achieve in five years' time.

老闆非常清楚他 5 年內想要達到的目標。

10. **far from / by no means clear** 非常不清楚的

The directions he gave me were <u>far from clear</u>.

他給的指示很不清楚。

11. **out of a clear blue sky**

突然、突如其來（= out of the blue）

The invasion came <u>out of a clear blue sky</u> and caught everyone off guard.

突如其來的入侵讓所有人都措手不及。

12. 「**clear** ＋一段時間」 指一段連續完整的時間；指一段空閒的時間

This application needs at least <u>three clear days</u> for delivery.

遞送這項申請至少需要整整 3 天。

I'm keeping <u>next week clear</u> for our honeymoon trip.

我為了我們的蜜月旅行把下星期空了下來。

Compelling 強而有説服力的、有趣的、強烈的

▶ MP3-024

compelling reason / argument 令人信服的理由、論點

I will stick with what I am doing now until I have a <u>compelling reason</u> to make changes.
除非我找到強烈的原因需要做改變，我會持續我現在所做的。

compelling evidence 令人信服的證據

Any strategy that deviates from this principle should require extraordinarily <u>compelling evidence</u>.
任何背離這個策略的準則都應該要有令人信服的證據。

compelling story 引人入勝的故事

It's a truly <u>compelling story</u> filled with well-researched elements that bring to life the story and characters.
這個十分吸引人的故事，因為做過詳盡的研究，使得故事和人物活靈活現。

compelling urge / desire / need 強烈的衝動、願望、需求

She felt a <u>compelling desire</u> to tell someone her plan to launch a new business.
她迫不及待想把她的創業計畫告訴別人。

Competitive 競爭力強的、有競爭力的、

激烈的 ▶ MP3-025

competitive edge 競爭力

The team seems to have lost its competitive edge recently.
這支隊伍近來喪失了競爭優勢。

competitive sports 競技體育

Children should be encouraged to engage in competitive sports, which encourage them to work together as a team.
我們應該鼓勵孩子從事競技體育，競技體育可以鼓勵他們團隊合作。

competitive salary 優渥、有競爭力的薪資

This company provides its employees with competitive salary and golden opportunities for career development.
這個公司提供員工優渥的薪資待遇和大好的職涯發展機會。

competitive advantage 競爭優勢

What would you say is your competitive advantage?
你認為你的競爭優勢是什麼呢？

Comprehensive 全面的、綜合的、詳盡的 ▶ MP3-026

comprehensive account / description 詳盡的描述

He wrote a fairly <u>comprehensive account</u> of the island.
他對這座島詳加描述。

comprehensive analysis / assessment / inspection / review 全面的分析 / 評估 / 檢測 / 檢視

The researchers carried out a thorough and <u>comprehensive analysis</u> of the case.
研究人員對這個病例進行全面分析。

comprehensive approach 全面的方法

The minister promised a <u>comprehensive approach</u> to healthcare reform.
部長承諾會採取全面的醫療改革措施。

comprehensive database / directory / index / list / listing 詳盡的資料庫 / 名錄 / 索引 / 清單

You can follow this link for a <u>comprehensive listing</u> of all the local activities.
你可以從這個連結取得一張列有當地所有活動的詳盡清單。

comprehensive collection / package / portfolio / set 綜合的套組

They offer a <u>comprehensive</u> benefits <u>package</u> to provide better care for people with disabilities.
他們提出一個綜合福利計畫，提供殘疾人士更好的照顧。

comprehensive cover / coverage / insurance / policy 綜合的保險

If you are an inexperienced driver, it is worth having <u>comprehensive insurance</u>.
如果你是沒有經驗的駕駛人，就值得投保綜合險。

comprehensive coverage / report 詳盡的報導

Clearly, students will need more <u>comprehensive coverage</u> of particular periods, but as a general introduction this book is excellent.
學生很明顯需要有針對特定時期更詳盡的報導，但以一本概論來說，這書已經很棒了。

comprehensive defeat / victory 全面的失敗 / 勝利

The army won a <u>comprehensive victory</u> that ended the civil war.
軍隊獲得全面勝利，結束了這場內戰。

comprehensive education / system 綜合的教育 / 體系

We will discuss two different methods that have the advantage that they can be combined into a more comprehensive system.
我們將討論兩種不同的方法，好處是它們能構成一個更全面的體系。

comprehensive guide / handbook 詳盡的手冊、指南

She has written a fully comprehensive guide to Asia.
她寫了一本詳盡的亞洲旅遊指南。

comprehensive information 詳盡的資訊

We don't have comprehensive information to make a decision at the present time.
我們目前沒有詳盡的資訊可以做決定。

comprehensive investigation / research / study / survey 詳盡的研究、調查

The report includes a comprehensive survey of the company's training needs.
這份報告包含了公司培訓需求的詳盡調查。

comprehensive knowledge / picture 詳盡的了解

The manager has a comprehensive knowledge of the Japanese market.
經理充分了解日本市場。

They still do not have a comprehensive picture of what happened.
他們對發生的事情還沒有充分了解。

comprehensive overview 綜合的概述

That book is a comprehensive overview of European history since the Renaissance.
那本書是歐洲歷史自文藝復興開始的綜合概述。

comprehensive plan / program 全面的計畫

The committee offered a comprehensive plan for redevelopment and conservation in all areas of the city.
委員會提出了一項全面的都市重建和保存計畫。

comprehensive range 廣泛的範圍

We offer our customers a comprehensive range of financial products.
我們提供顧客全方位的金融產品。

comprehensive service 全面的服務

Our professional staff members provide a <u>comprehensive service</u> for athletes.
我們的專業人員為運動選手提供全面的服務。

comprehensive training 綜合的訓練

We offer you <u>comprehensive training</u> in all aspects of the field.
我們會提供你這個領域的綜合訓練。

comprehensive view 全面的觀點

We need to take a more <u>comprehensive view</u> of the issue.
我們必須用更全面的觀點來看這個議題。

Concerted 共同的、協力一致的 ▶ MP3-027

concerted action / campaign 共同的行動

Richer countries of the world should take <u>concerted action</u> to help poorer countries.
世界上較富裕的國家應該共同採取行動來幫助較貧困的國家。

concerted attack 聯合的攻擊

The country is not capable of defending itself against a <u>concerted attack</u> from the western countries.
該國無力抵擋來自西方國家的聯合攻擊。

concerted attempt / effort 共同嘗試 / 努力

The organizations have made a <u>concerted effort</u> to raise the standards of education.
這些組織共同致力於提高教育水平。

Considerable 相當大的、相當多的

▶ MP3-028

considerable amount / number / sum

大量（amount / sum 修飾不可數名詞；number 修飾可數名詞）

A <u>considerable amount</u> of time and effort has gone into this exhibition.
這次的展覽花了相當多的時間和精力。

considerable attention / concern 相當多的注意 / 關注

Drug trafficking is a matter of <u>considerable concern</u> for the entire country.
毒品走私是整個國家相當關注的問題。

considerable damage 重大的損害

The fire caused <u>considerable damage</u> to the museum.
那場火災嚴重損害博物館。

considerable degree / extent / level 很大的程度

Catholicism has influenced the architecture to a <u>considerable extent</u>.
天主教深深影響這個建築風格。

considerable delay 嚴重的延遲

There was a <u>considerable delay</u> in the process of our application.
我們的申請流程嚴重延遲。

considerable demand 相當多的需求、要求

There's always a <u>considerable demand</u> for milk in summer.
夏天的鮮奶需求量總是相當大。

considerable discomfort 嚴重的不適

You may experience <u>considerable discomfort</u> after the operation in the first few days.
手術後的頭幾天，你可能會感到嚴重不適。

considerable effect / impact / influence 重大的影響

The recent slowdown in the US economy is likely to have a <u>considerable impact</u> on the rest of the world.
最近美國經濟衰退可能會對全世界造成重大影響。

considerable effort 相當大的努力

It takes constant and <u>considerable effort</u> to master a language.
要精通一種語言需要持續且大量的努力。

considerable importance 相當重要

These findings have <u>considerable</u> archaeological
<u>importance</u>.
這些發現在考古學上極為重要。

considerable interest 相當大的興趣

The series of works have aroused <u>considerable interest</u>
among people.
這一系列的作品已經引起民眾極大的興趣。

considerable risk 相當大的風險

There are <u>considerable risks</u> inherent in the policy.
這項政策存在相當大的風險。

considerable variation 相當大的差異

<u>Considerable variations</u> were found in the terms offered by
different banks.
不同銀行提供的條款有相當大的差異。

Decent 正派的、得體的、相當好的 ▶ MP3-029

decent job 不錯的工作

He hopes to land a <u>decent job</u> after graduating from college.
他希望大學畢業後找到一個不錯的工作。

decent pay 合理像樣的薪水

Workers should all be treated with dignity and respect, and at the very least get <u>decent pay</u>.
勞工應該都要受到尊重和尊敬，以及至少獲得合理像樣的工資。

decent restaurant 像樣的餐廳

I suggest that you take your parents to a <u>decent</u> Japanese <u>restaurant</u>.
我建議你帶你的父母去一個像樣的日本料理餐廳。

decent citizen / person 正派的市民、人

The majority of the residents in this neighborhood are fairly <u>decent citizen</u>.
大部分住在這個地方的居民都是相當正派的市民。

Deep 深的；（程度）深的、極度的 ▶ MP3-030

deep affection / feeling / love 深厚的感情

In order to maintain a long-married life, what is needed is not a marriage certificate but the <u>deep affection</u> between husbands and wives.
要維持一段長久的婚姻，靠的並不是一張結婚證書，而是夫妻之間深厚的感情。

deep breath / sigh 深呼吸 / 深深嘆息

As he heard the news, he gave a <u>deep sigh</u> and dropped into silence.
聽到消息，他深深嘆了一口氣後陷入沉默。

deep darkness 漆黑

The street was in <u>deep darkness</u>; people did not know what they stumbled over.
整條街一片漆黑，民眾自己絆到了什麼都不清楚。

deep depression / disappointment / regret / sympathy 極度沮喪 / 失望 / 後悔 / 同情

She is in a state of <u>deep depression</u> on account of losing the game.

她因為輸了比賽而深感沮喪。

We expressed our <u>deep sympathy</u> to Japan for the tragic loss of lives caused by the earthquake.

我們對日本大地震奪走的性命深表同情。

deep discount 大折扣

Some companies are offering <u>deep discounts</u> to attract shoppers.

有些公司提供很大的折扣來吸引顧客。

deep discussion 深入的討論

The professor is having a <u>deep discussion</u> on the issue with students.

教授和學生正在深入討論這個議題。

deep divisions 嚴重的分歧

Despite the peace process, there are <u>deep divisions</u> in the community.

儘管有和平進程，社區中仍存在著嚴重分歧。

deep impression 深刻的印象

What she said made a <u>deep impression</u> on me.
她說的話讓我印象深刻。

deep recession 嚴重的蕭條

The war plunged the country into a <u>deep recession</u>.
戰爭使這個國家陷入嚴重的經濟蕭條。

deep sleep 熟睡

The baby lay in bed and fell into a <u>deep sleep</u>.
小嬰兒在床上睡得很熟。

deep understanding 深刻的理解

For some simple cases, a <u>deep understanding</u> of these concepts is not necessarily required.
對於一些簡單的狀況，不一定要深刻了解這些概念才能處理。

實用短語 / 用法 / 句型　　　▶ MP3-031

1. **to be deep in debt** 身陷債務之中
   After my surgery, we <u>were deep in debt</u> with exorbitant bills.
   手術之後，我們身陷大筆的醫療債務當中。

2. to be deep in thought

深入交談 / 陷入沉思（而沒有注意到周遭的事）

The professor <u>is deep in thought</u> with eyes fixed on the far end of the room.

教授眼睛盯著房間的遠方發呆，陷入沉思。

3. to be in / get into deep water

處於困境（也可以説 to be in deep trouble）

The party <u>is in deep water</u> over its plans for tax increases.

這個政黨因為他們的增稅計畫而陷入水深火熱之中。

4. to go off the deep end　莽撞衝動行事；勃然大怒

You'd better think it over and don't <u>go off the deep end</u>.

你最好多加考慮，不要衝動行事。

One minute we were having a perfectly reasonable discussion and the next minute he just <u>went off the deep end</u>!

前一秒我們還在進行合理的討論，他下一秒卻暴怒！

5. to jump into the deep end　獨自應付難題

I'm a little nervous about starting my graduate degree, but I'm determined to <u>jump into the deep end</u>.

我對研究所感到有點緊張，但我還是決定要放手一搏。

Deep-rooted 根深蒂固的

▶ MP3-032

（1. 也有「deeply-rooted」的寫法　2. 意思和「deep-seated」相似）

deep-rooted belief / faith　根深蒂固的想法 / 信念

The study challenges a <u>deep-rooted belief</u> that fish oil has benefits for people.
這項研究質疑一直以來深信魚油對人體有益的看法。

deep-rooted fear　根深蒂固的恐懼

The girl is gripped by <u>deep-rooted fears</u> and they will not subside.
這個小女孩受根深蒂固的恐懼所困擾，而這些恐懼揮之不去。

deep-rooted prejudice　根深蒂固的偏見

The concept originates from <u>deep-rooted prejudice</u> on matters of race, religion and culture.
這個概念來自對種族、宗教、文化根深蒂固的偏見。

deep-rooted problem　根深蒂固的問題

More things need to be done to tackle <u>deep-rooted</u> social <u>problems</u>.
要解決根深蒂固的社會問題，還需要做更多的事情。

deep-rooted racism 根深蒂固的種族主義

This incident brought to light what some see as <u>deep-rooted racism</u> in the country.

這個事件揭露了在這個國家根深蒂固的種族主義。

Difficult 困難的、艱難的；難相處的　▶ MP3-033

difficult time　艱難的時期

That will be the way to get the economy through this <u>difficult time</u>.
那會是使經濟擺脫這段艱難時期的方法。

difficult customer　難搞的顧客

My colleague gave me some tips to deal with <u>difficult customers</u>.
我的同事給了我一些對付難搞顧客的建議。

實用短語 / 用法 / 句型　▶ MP3-034

1. **to make life / things difficult for sb**
   使某人的生活 / 事情變得困難、為難某人
   This strategy is <u>making life difficult for</u> asylum-seekers.
   這個政策使難民的生活變得困難。

2. **notoriously difficult**
   眾所皆知的困難（大家都知道～非常困難）
   That man is <u>notoriously difficult</u> to get along with.
   大家都知道那個人非常難相處。

3. **technically difficult** 技術上、執行上困難

The stage lighting is not <u>technically difficult</u>, but overly expensive.

這樣的舞台燈光執行上並不難,但成本過高。

補充 雖然「tough」和「difficult」的意思相近,但形容人時,「difficult」有「難相處的」意思,「tough」則有「堅強的」和「難相處的」兩種解釋。

Downright 完全的、徹底的

▶ MP3-035

downright fool 徹底的笨蛋

He had taken me for a <u>downright fool</u>.
他完全把我當成笨蛋。

downright hostility 徹底的敵意

The two parties are far too often seeing each other suspiciously or with <u>downright hostility</u>.
兩黨經常對彼此抱有懷疑的態度或是徹底的敵意。

downright lie 徹底的謊言

What he just said is a <u>downright lie</u>!
他剛剛說的全是謊言！

實用短語 / 用法 / 句型（補充副詞用法） ▶ MP3-036

1. **downright crazy** 極度瘋狂的
   This idea may sound <u>downright crazy</u> now, but we can give it a go.
   這個想法現在聽起來可能非常瘋狂，但我們可以試試看。

2. **downright dangerous** 極度危險的

The idea, if put into practice, would be <u>downright dangerous</u>.

這個想法如果付諸行動會非常危險。

3. **downright illegal** 完全不合法的

The trade remained popular, though <u>downright illegal</u>, until the 20th century.

儘管完全不合法，這交易一直到 20 世紀都非常受歡迎。

4. **downright impossible** 完全不可能的

The project is extremely difficult, if not <u>downright impossible</u>.

就算有可能，這計畫也是極度困難。

5. **downright mean** 極度卑鄙的

I thought it was <u>downright mean</u> of him not to lend me the car.

我覺得他不借我車實在太惡劣了。

6. **downright ridiculous / stupid**

極度荒謬的 / 愚蠢的

It's <u>downright ridiculous</u> that the office isn't open on Mondays!

辦公室星期一沒開實在太荒謬了！

7. **downright rude** 極度無禮的

I find this extremely unprofessional, not to mention <u>downright rude</u>.

我覺得這非常不專業，更別說是極度無禮了。

Drastic 劇烈的；嚴厲的

▶ MP3-037

drastic change / improvement / shift 大幅改變

Drastic changes are needed if environmental catastrophes are to be avoided.
如果要避免環境災難，就需要徹底的改變。

drastic cut / reduction 大幅削減

Many employees have to take drastic cuts in pay this year.
許多員工今年不得不接受大幅減薪。

drastic effect 劇烈的影響

The piece of news has had a drastic effect on membership and many clubs are finding it increasingly difficult to make ends meet.
這則新聞對健身房會員數造成很大的影響，許多健身房越來越難經營。

drastic action / measures / step 嚴厲的措施、手段

Drastic measures are needed to clean up the profession.
整頓這個行業需要採取嚴厲的手段。

Easy 容易的；舒適的、自在的、放心的 ▶ MP3-038

easy money （以不法手段）得來容易的錢、不義之財

The thought of <u>easy money</u> draws many teenagers to drug dealing.
賺輕鬆錢的想法吸引了很多年輕人從事毒品交易。

easy pickings 易取得、易竊取的東西

A solo traveler equals <u>easy pickings</u> for a seasoned criminal.
獨自旅行的遊客是慣竊下手的好目標。

easy prey 易下手的獵物

No matter what country tourists are in, they are <u>easy prey</u> for thieves.
不論在哪個國家，遊客都很容易成為小偷的獵物。

easy target 輕鬆的、容易攻擊的目標

Famous landmarks are <u>easy targets</u> for terrorists.
著名地標很容易成為恐怖分子攻擊的目標。

easy ride 輕鬆的過程、一路順利

It seems like half of the job is done, but the rest is not an <u>easy ride</u>.
工作似乎已經完成一半了，但剩下的部分並不輕鬆。

1. to be easy on the ear / eye 好聽的 / 好看的

Her handwriting <u>is</u> very <u>easy on the eye</u>.
她的字很好看。

2. to be / live on easy street

如果說一個人 be / live on easy street，代表某人過著富裕的生活

When he gets this contract signed, he'll <u>live on easy street</u>.
一旦簽了這份約，他的生活就會變得富裕。

3. to go easy on sb 善待某人、對某人不嚴苛

The judges <u>went easy on</u> the criminals because they were teenagers.
因為犯人是青少年，法官對他們比較不嚴苛。

4. to go easy on sth 節制使用某物

The doctor told me to <u>go easy on</u> the spicy food for a while.
醫生要我暫時少吃點辛辣的食物。

5. to have an easy time (of it) 過得輕鬆自在

Now that the kids have all left home, the parents can <u>have an easy time of it</u>.
現在小孩都已經長大離家，父母可以過得輕鬆了。

6. **to take the easy way out**

以最省事、簡單的方法解決困境，但不一定是最適當的方法

Many people <u>take the easy way out</u> of financial trouble by declaring bankruptcy.
許多人利用宣布破產來擺脫財務困境。

7. **(as) easy as pie / abc / falling off a log**

非常容易的

For me, getting a driver license is <u>as easy as pie</u>.
對我來說，要拿到駕照非常容易。

8. **easier said than done** 説的比做的簡單

To not be emotional in that situation is <u>easier said than done</u>.
在那種情況下要不激動，説的比做的簡單。

9. **easy to be with** 好相處的

He is gentle and <u>easy to be with</u>.
他人很和善又好相處。

10. **it's / that's easy for you to say**

你説的倒容易（口語的反諷用法）

<u>It's easy for you to say</u> that, but actually it is not so simple.
你説的倒容易，但事情哪有那麼簡單。

11. **on easy terms**

以分期付款的方式（= in installments）

He bought a set of furniture <u>on easy terms</u>.
他分期付款買了一套傢俱。

12. there are no easy answers 沒有簡單的解決方法

There are no easy answers to this financial problem.

沒有簡單的方法能解決這個財務問題。

13. within easy driving / walking distance

開車 / 走路就可以到的、距離不遠的

The beach is within easy walking distance of the hotel.

海灘從飯店走路就可以到達。

14. within easy reach 在附近、唾手可得的

The man likes to keep a dictionary within easy reach when he's writing.

這人在寫作的時候喜歡把字典放在手邊。

Effective 有效的、（法律、制度）生效的

effective drug 有效的藥物

Cheaper <u>drugs</u> are not necessarily less <u>effective</u> than the more expensive ones.
便宜的藥物不一定比昂貴的藥物沒有效。

rules to be effective 規則生效

These new <u>rules</u> introduced by the interim CEO will <u>be effective</u> next week.
這些中繼的執行長所制定的新規則將在下個星期生效。

effective remedy 有效的挽救方法

We have to resign ourselves to fate since we have trouble coming up with an <u>effective remedy</u>.
既然我們想不出一個有效的挽救方式，那麼就只能聽天由命了。

effective speech 有效的演講

An <u>effective</u> persuasive <u>speech</u> typically includes a synopsis of the evidence presented above.
一篇有效的說服性演講，通常會包含上述所舉證據的總結。

Empty 空的、無人的；空虛的、空洞的、無意義的

▶ MP3-041

empty space 空白的空間

I'm used to leaving a large empty space at the bottom of my notes.

我習慣在筆記下方留下很大的空白。

empty life 空虛的生活

He said his life had been completely empty since his wife died.

他說自從他老婆過世，他的生活就變得完全沒有意義。

empty gesture / promise / word 空話、空頭支票

His repeated promises to pay me back were just empty words.

他再三保證會還我錢，結果都只是空話。

empty rhetoric 浮誇的言詞

The politician's speech was just empty rhetoric.

這個政客的演講盡是浮誇之詞。

empty suit 虛有其表的政客、專業人士

He acts like a big shot, but he is just an empty suit.

他裝得像是個大人物，但他只是虛有其表。

empty threat 虛張聲勢的威脅

His father threatened to throw him out, but he knew that it was an <u>empty threat</u>.

他爸爸威脅要趕他出去，但他知道那只是在嚇唬他。

實用短語 / 用法 / 句型 ▶ MP3-042

1. **to be running on empty** 精疲力盡

   I get the impression she's <u>been running on empty</u> for days now.

   我覺得幾天下來她已經累壞了。

2. **empty-handed** 空手的

   Delegates from the warring sides held a new round of peace talks but went away <u>empty-handed</u>.

   交戰各方代表舉行了新的和平談判，但卻空手而歸。

3. **empty-headed** 沒腦袋的、傻的

   Many people had wrongly assumed she was nothing more than a beautiful but <u>empty-headed</u> woman.

   很多人都誤以為她只是個沒有腦袋的美女。

4. **on an empty stomach** 空腹的、餓肚子的

   You should not go to work <u>on an empty stomach</u>.

   你不應該餓肚子去上班。

Exhaustive 全面的、徹底的、詳盡的

▶ MP3-043

exhaustive account / description 詳盡的描述

There are plenty of books that offer an <u>exhaustive description</u> of those events.
很多書對那些事件都有詳盡的描述。

exhaustive analysis / examination / review / search 徹底的分析 / 檢查 / 檢視 / 搜尋

The rescue team conducted an <u>exhaustive search</u> of the area.
搜救隊徹底搜尋了這個區域。

exhaustive checklist / list / listing 詳盡的清單

This is by no means an <u>exhaustive list</u> but it gives an indication of many projects taking place.
這絕對不是個詳盡的清單，但從它能看出很多計劃正在進行。

exhaustive detail 詳盡的細節

The guide outlines every bus route in <u>exhaustive detail</u>.
這本指南詳細說明每一條公車路線。

exhaustive inquiry / investigation / research / study / survey 徹底的調查、研究

This information was gained after an <u>exhaustive investigation</u> by the Dutch government.
荷蘭政府做了徹底的調查後取得了這個訊息。

Exorbitant （價格、要求）過高的、過分的、

離譜的

exorbitant amount / sum 高得離譜的金額

The agent successfully sold the building for an <u>exorbitant sum</u>.
這個房仲成功用天價把那棟大樓賣出去了。

exorbitant charge / cost / fee / rates 過高的費用

We were charged <u>exorbitant rates</u> for phone calls.
我們被收取過高的通話費用。

exorbitant demand 過分的要求

The project suffered as a result of <u>exorbitant demands</u> made by landowners.
這項計畫因為地主過分的要求而受阻。

exorbitant price 過高的價格

<u>Exorbitant</u> housing <u>prices</u> have created an acute shortage of affordable housing for youngsters.
過高的房價造成年輕人經濟能力負擔得起的住宅嚴重短缺。

Fair 公正的、公平的；合理的；相當大的；晴朗的

▶ MP3-045

fair comment 公正的評論

He claims his article was a <u>fair comment</u> on a matter of public interest.
他聲稱他的文章是就大眾利益寫的公正評論。

fair deal 公平的交易、待遇

Nurses took to the streets to get a <u>fair deal</u> from the government.
為了得到政府公平的待遇，護士走上街頭。

fair trial 公平的審判

When people break the law, they are supposed to be guaranteed a <u>fair trial</u>.
當人民違法，他們理應受到公平的審判。

fair guess / idea 合理的猜測 / 想法

It's a <u>fair guess</u> to say that increasing tax will lead to some changes in people's lifestyle.
認為增稅會造成民眾生活方式改變，是一個合理的猜測。

fair price 合理的價格

I thought it was a <u>fair price</u> that they were offering.
我認為他們的報價是合理的。

fair question 合理的問題

That's a <u>fair question</u>, and it deserves an honest reply.
那是個合理的問題，應該要誠實回答。

fair wage 合理的薪水

The workers demanded a <u>fair wage</u> for their work.
工人要求合理的工資。

fair amount / bit / number 相當大的數量（amount / bit 修飾不可數名詞；number 修飾可數名詞）

We spent a <u>fair amount</u> of time thinking about what might go wrong in this program.
我們花了很多時間在思考這個學程可能出了什麼問題。

fair chance 很大的可能

There's a <u>fair chance</u> we'll be coming over to Taiwan this summer.
今年夏天我們很有可能會去台灣。

fair distance / way 相當遠的距離

Our cousins live a <u>fair distance</u> away so we don't see them very often.
我們的堂兄弟住得很遠，所以我們不常見到面。

fair weather 晴朗的天氣

In <u>fair weather</u>, we could go for a picnic in Central Park.
天氣好的時候，我們可以去中央公園野餐。

實用短語 / 用法 / 句型　▶ MP3-046

1. **to have one's fair share of sth**
   遭遇許多不好的事情
   He's <u>had his fair share of</u> tragedies in his career life.
   他的職業生涯中遭遇過太多不幸。

2. **a fair crack of the whip**　平等的機會
   It's only fair that all the candidates should be given <u>a fair crack of the whip</u>.
   每個候選人都應該享有平等的機會才合理。

3. **by fair means or foul**　不擇手段
   They were determined to win the game, <u>by fair means or foul</u>.
   他們下定決心不擇手段都要贏得比賽。

4. **fair is fair**　公平、公正一點
   It's not because I'm greedy. <u>Fair is fair</u>, she certainly earns half of the money.
   不是我貪心。說句公道話，她確實賺了一半的錢。

5. **fair enough** 有道理的、説得對

That is <u>fair enough</u>. We should start the project right now in the hope of an improvement.

這話講得很有道理，我們應該現在開始這項計畫，希望能有所改善。

6. **fair go** 公道一些；公平的機會

Everyone in this country has the right to a <u>fair go</u>, without discrimination.

這個國家的每個人都應有平等的機會，不受任何歧視。

7. **it is fair to say** 可以這麼説、這麼説是合理的

I think <u>it's fair to say</u> you've done the best you could.

我認為你已經盡力了。

8. **to be fair** 説句公道話、憑良心説

He should have phoned to tell us what his plans were, although, <u>to be fair</u>, he's been very busy.

憑良心説，他雖然一直很忙，但應該也要打通電話告訴我們他的計畫是什麼。

Fast 快速的；放蕩的；牢固的

▶ MP3-047

fast lane 快車道

In a rush for his daughter's birthday party, Kevin took the fast lane back to the city.
為了要趕上女兒的生日派對，凱文開快車道回都市。

fast talker 能言善道的人

He is a fast talker, which might explain why he is successful in politics.
他能言善道，這或許能解釋為什麼他在政治上如此成功。

fast life

放蕩、充滿刺激和危險的生活（也可以說 life in the fast lane）

Life in Detroit no longer satisfied him; he wanted the fast life in California.
底特律的生活不再能滿足他了，他想要加州那種充滿刺激的生活。

實用短語 / 用法 / 句型　　　▶ MP3-048

1. **to hold / stand fast (+ to)** 堅定不移、堅持某事
   We can only try to hold fast to the age-old values—honesty is the best policy.
   我們只能試著堅信長久以來不變的價值觀：誠實為上策。

He told supporters to <u>stand fast</u> over the next few vital days.

他要支持者在接下來關鍵的幾天堅持信念。

2. to make a fast / quick buck

快速賺得一大筆錢，通常是靠不正當的方式快速獲利

The employee illegally changed the financial records of the company and <u>made a fast buck</u>.

員工違法篡改了公司的財務紀錄，這讓他在短時間內撈了一大筆錢。

3. to play fast and loose

輕率地對待、玩弄（某人 / 某事）

Like many movie-makers, he <u>plays fast and loose</u> with the facts to tell his own version of the story.

他和許多電影製作人一樣，對事實並不在乎，喜歡用自己的角度來説故事。

4. to pull a fast one (+ on sb)　欺騙某人

You paid too much for that. I think they <u>pulled a fast one on</u> you.

那個東西不值那麼多錢，我覺得你上了他們的當。

5. fast asleep　熟睡的

When he went upstairs five minutes later, his girlfriend was <u>fast asleep</u>.

5 分鐘之後，他走上樓，這時女朋友已經睡得很熟了。

6. 「時間＋ fast」時鐘或手錶的時間快了多少時間

My watch is <u>ten minutes fast</u>.

我手錶的時間快了 10 分鐘。

Fat 肥胖的;厚的;(利潤、費用)豐厚的;極少的

▶ MP3-049

fat cat 肥貓(原指有錢有勢的人物或大老闆,後來比喻企業裡坐領高薪卻不用做事的人,帶有貶義)

The employees criticized the <u>fat cats</u> who award themselves huge pay increases in the company.
員工批評公司裡的肥貓為自己大幅加薪。

fat book 厚重的書

As English majors, we have to bring the <u>fat books</u> to the literature class every week.
身為英語系學生,我們每個星期都要抱著厚重的書去上文學課。

fat wallet
厚的錢包(因為錢包塞滿了鈔票,可以用來比喻一個人很有錢)

He took out his <u>fat wallet</u> and picked up the bill.
他拿出厚厚的錢包來買單。

fat check 巨額支票

We just received a big <u>fat check</u> from the international corporation.
我們剛剛收到這間跨國公司的巨額支票。

fat contract 肥約

The rookie just entered into a <u>fat contract</u> with the Golden State Warriors.
這個新秀剛和金州勇士隊簽了一份肥約。

fat profit 暴利

Some producers of mineral water have made <u>fat profits</u> in previous years.
有些礦泉水製造商在前幾年已經賺了一大筆錢。

fat chance 不太可能、機會渺茫（反諷用法）

"Perhaps they will invite you to the party."
"<u>Fat chance</u> (of that)!"

「或許他們會邀你去派對。」
「怎麼可能！」

實用短語 / 用法 / 句型　　　▶ MP3-050

1. **to chew the fat** 閒聊、打屁
   They sat in a bar just <u>chewing the fat</u> for the whole night.
   他們坐在酒吧閒聊了一整晚。

2. **to grow fat on sth** 因為某事而變得富有（貶義）
   These stock brokers <u>grow fat on</u> other people's money.
   這些證券經理人利用別人的錢賺錢。

Favorable 稱讚的、正面的；有利的、適合的

▶ MP3-051

favorable attitude / opinion 贊同的態度 / 看法

He formed a very <u>favorable opinion</u> of the city, which he spent a month exploring.
他很喜愛那個城市，在那裡玩了一個月。

favorable comment / review 好評

The series gained <u>favorable reviews</u> from the very first episode.
這齣劇從第一集就獲得好評。

favorable comparison 比得上

The film bears <u>favorable</u> technical <u>comparison</u> with Hollywood productions costing five times as much.
這部電影在技術上和好萊塢電影有得比，但製作成本卻只要它們的五分之一。

favorable coverage / report 正面的、有利的報導

State-run television channels offer some highly <u>favorable</u> <u>coverage</u> of the party.
國營電視台報導一些非常偏袒這個政黨的新聞。

favorable impression 好的、正面的印象

The ad has reached enough viewers to make a <u>favorable impression</u> across the country.
這支廣告已經觸及夠多的觀眾，讓他們對這個國家留下了好的印象。

favorable publicity 正面的宣傳

Now many companies attempt to get <u>favorable publicity</u> through product placement.
現在有很多公司試圖透過置入性行銷來獲得正面的宣傳效果。

favorable rating 正面的評價

The movie received a highly <u>favorable rating</u> on IMDb.
這部電影在 IMDb 上獲得很高的評價。

favorable reaction / reception / response
正面的、良好的回應

This newly opened Italian restaurant has already received a <u>favorable response</u> from critics.
這家新開幕的義大利餐廳已經深受美食家的好評。

favorable circumstances / conditions / environment / position / situation 有利的環境、形勢

The government aims to create <u>favorable conditions</u> for a strong and sustainable economy.
政府打算為強勁且可持續發展的經濟創造有利的環境。

favorable impact 有利的影響

The appreciation of the New Taiwan dollar has a <u>favorable impact</u> on importers.
新台幣升值有利於進口商。

favorable outcome / result 有利的結果

None of these actions guarantees a <u>favorable outcome</u>.
這些作為都無法保證會有一個好的結果。

favorable recommendation 有利的建議

The female author gives many <u>favorable recommendations</u> in her autobiography.
這位女作者在她的自傳中給了很多有利的建議。

favorable terms / treatment 有利的、優惠的條件 / 待遇

There are also companies that appear to have received <u>favorable treatment</u> in the list.
名單上的公司似乎也受到優惠待遇。

favorable weather 有利的、適合的天氣

Assisted by <u>favorable weather</u> conditions, the launch was successful.
受到有利天氣狀況的幫忙，這次的發射很成功。

Fertile 肥沃的、富饒的、能生育的、點子多的

▶ MP3-052

fertile imagination 豐富的想像力

J.K. Rowling is renowned as a novelist with a <u>fertile imagination</u>.
J.K. 羅琳以身為想像力豐富的作家聞名。

fertile mind / brain 豐富的想像力

Some people consider a <u>fertile mind</u> to be a prerequisite for being a successful novelist.
有些人認為擁有豐富的想像力是成為成功小說家的前提。

fertile land / ground / soil 肥沃的土地、土壤

The desert continually encroaches on the <u>fertile land</u>.
沙漠不斷地侵襲這片肥沃的土地。

fertile thoughts 豐富的思想、點子

According to the author, a creative mind will produce its most <u>fertile thoughts</u> in periods of full relaxation.
依此作者而言，人在完全放鬆的狀況下，富有創造力的腦會產生最豐富的點子。

Fine

好的、傑出的；（身體狀況）良好的；細微的、精確的、精緻的

▶ MP3-053

fine figure of a man / woman

身材健壯的男人 / 身材姣好的女人

In her portrait, Beckham is a <u>fine figure of a man</u>.
在她的描述中，貝克漢是個身材很好的男人。

fine mess 一團糟、困境（反諷用法）

That's another <u>fine mess</u> he's got himself into.
那是他自己陷入的另一個困境。

fine performance 精彩的演出

That <u>fine performance</u> dispelled any doubts about his abilities.
那場精彩演出消除了任何對他能力的質疑。

fine wine 好酒

The restaurant was famous for its gourmet food and <u>fine wines</u>.
這家餐廳以其美食和美酒聞名。

fine adjustment 微調

After a close examination, the mechanic made <u>fine adjustments</u> to the engine.
經過一番仔細檢查，技師對引擎做了微調。

fine craftsmanship 精巧的手藝

We admired the fine craftsmanship of the furniture.
我們欽佩這個傢俱的精湛工藝。

fine detail / point 具體的細節

I understood in general what he was talking about, but some of the finer details were beyond me.
我大概了解他在說什麼，但是有一些更具體的細節不是很清楚。

fine distinction 細微的差別

There is only a fine distinction between misrepresenting the truth and lying.
扭曲事實和說謊之間只有細微差別。

fine features 精緻的面容

Her dark hair accentuates her fine features.
深色的頭髮襯托了她精緻的面容。

fine feelings 細膩的情感

As a leader, he has a knack for appealing to people's fine feelings.
身為一個領導人，他很了解如何喚起民眾細膩的情感。

fine line 一線之隔

There is a <u>fine line</u> between vulgar and sexy, and it's been crossed too often.
低俗和性感只有一線之隔，兩者常被混為一談。

fine print 附屬細則（印刷得極小的字體，通常是合約或正式文件中，業者希望消費者忽略掉的附屬條款）

Make sure that you read the <u>fine print</u> before you sign the contract.
在簽合約之前一定要看清楚附屬細則。

實用短語 / 用法 / 句型　　▶ MP3-054

1. **to be in fine form** 處於良好的狀態
   Thomas <u>was in fine form</u>, scoring 40 points, and his team took a 3-0 series lead.
   湯瑪斯的狀況良好，單場比賽拿下 40 分，球隊取得 3 比 0 的領先。

2. **to get / have sth down to a fine art**
   將某事物發揮得淋漓盡致，因為已經反覆做了無數次
   The chef has <u>got</u> brunch <u>down to a fine art</u>.
   這位大廚做的早午餐無懈可擊。

3. **not to put too fine a point on it** 不客氣地説、坦白説
   His performance, <u>not to put too fine a point on it</u>, was terrible.
   不客氣地説，他的表現很糟。

Firm 穩固的；確定、確切的；嚴格、強硬的；堅定、堅決的

▶ MP3-055

firm base / basis / foothold / foundation 穩固的基礎

The firm has established a <u>firm foothold</u> in the British market.
這間公司在英國市場站穩了腳步。

firm control 牢牢控制

They insist on maintaining a <u>firm control</u> over the project.
他們堅持要維持對這個計畫的全權控制。

firm friends 親近的朋友

Kevin and Peter have been <u>firm friends</u> since childhood.
凱文和彼得從小就是好朋友。

firm date 確切的日期

Can you set a <u>firm date</u> for the meeting?
你能定一下開會的確切日期嗎？

firm decision 確定的、不能改變的決定

Our clients haven't reached a <u>firm decision</u> on that matter yet.
我們的客戶還沒對那事做出確切的決定。

firm evidence 確切的證據

Now the prosecutor has <u>firm evidence</u> of this criminal activity.
檢方現在已經掌握了犯罪活動的確切證據。

firm grasp / grip 充分理解

To do the job well, you need a <u>firm grasp</u> of how international banking works.
要做好這份工作，你需要對國際銀行業的運作方式有充分了解。

firm handshake 堅定有力的握手

Giving a <u>firm handshake</u> may create a favorable first impression.
堅定有力的握手可能會給人一個好的第一印象。

firm leadership 強硬的領導

What the company needs most now is <u>firm leadership</u>.
公司現在最需要的是強硬的領導。

firm advocate / believer / supporter

堅定的支持者、堅信的人

We're <u>firm believers</u> in healthy eating and regular exercise.
我們堅信健康飲食和規律運動的重要。

firm belief / conviction 堅定的信念、立場（= firmly believe）

It is my <u>firm belief</u> that we must encourage debate.
我堅信我們應該鼓勵辯論。

firm commitment 堅定的承諾

The president gave a <u>firm commitment</u> that the economy would get better.
總統堅決保證經濟會好轉。

firm stance / stand 堅定的立場

We should take a <u>firm stand</u> on this issue.
我們應該對這爭議採取堅定的立場。

實用短語 / 用法 / 句型　　▶ MP3-056

1. **to be on firm ground**
   對某事確定、有充分的事實為依據
   She <u>was on firm ground</u>, for she had pondered this matter for months.
   她對這事很確定，因為她已經思考好幾個月了。

2. 「**a firm grasp / grip + of**」有「充分的理解」的意思，但「**a firm grip + on**」則是「牢牢抓住；牢牢控制」
   Mother kept <u>a firm grip on</u> my hand as we crossed the street.
   我們過馬路時，媽媽緊緊抓著我的手。

Flat
平坦的、扁平的；（容器）淺的；（飲料）沒氣的；（輪胎、球）洩氣的；（電池）沒電的；緊貼的；平淡的、缺乏熱情的；斷然的、肯定的；（金額）固定不變的；（市場、交易）蕭條的、不理想的；恰好的

▶ MP3-057

flat sea / water 平靜的水面

Light from the street light reflected on the flat, still water.
街燈的光映在平靜的水面上。

flat shoes 平底鞋

We wore slacks, sweaters, flat shoes, and all manner of casual attire for travel.
我們穿休閒褲、毛衣、平底鞋和各種休閒服裝出遊。

flat beer / drink / soda 沒氣的啤酒 / 飲料 / 汽水

If you don't put the top back on that bottle of soda, it will go flat.
如果你不把汽水的瓶蓋蓋上，它會沒氣。

flat tire 沒氣的輪胎

Unfortunately, we got a flat tire on our way to the airport.
我們在往機場的路上不幸爆胎了。

flat battery 沒電的電池

His car headlight was on for a whole day and, as a result, the battery went flat.
他的車頭燈亮了一整天，結果電瓶就沒電了。

flat voice 平淡的語氣

His voice was flat, with no passion or hope in it.
他的語氣很平淡，沒有一絲的熱情和希望。

flat denial 矢口否認

The official has issued a flat denial of the accusations against him.
官員矢口否認對他的指控。

flat refusal 斷然拒絕

His request for time off work was met with a flat refusal.
他請假的請求被斷然拒絕。

flat fee / rate 均一的費用

We charge a flat rate of NT$ 2,000 annually.
我們每年統一收取新台幣 2,000 元。

flat tax 單一稅（不論收入多少，均用同一稅率計算的稅收制度，累進稅則可以說 progressive tax）

The administration rejected a <u>flat tax</u> because it shifted too much of the tax burden from the rich to the poor.
政府否決了單一稅，因為它將過多的稅收負擔從富人轉嫁到窮人身上。

flat sales 銷售量平平、不理想

Analysts are expecting <u>flat sales</u> in the coming months.
分析師預計，未來幾個月的銷售量將平平。

實用短語 / 用法 / 句型 ▶ MP3-058

1. **to be flat on one's back** 臥病在床；平躺
   I've <u>been flat on my back</u> with the flu for two weeks.
   我已經感冒臥病在床兩個星期了。

2. **to fall flat** （笑話、主意、建議）未達預期效果
   Most of his jokes <u>fell flat</u> and his act was a disaster.
   他的笑話大多都不好笑，表演也爛透了。

3. **to fall flat on one's face** 一敗塗地、失敗
   If we don't get any funding, this building project will <u>fall flat on its face</u>.
   如果我們沒拿到任何資金，這個建築計畫將會失敗。

4. **(as) flat as a pancake** 非常平的

The land in that area is <u>as flat as a pancake</u>.

那裡的地非常平坦。

5. **flat against sth** 緊貼某物的

We should push the wardrobe <u>flat against</u> the wall.

我們要把衣櫃推到底，讓它緊貼牆壁。

6. **that's flat** 沒得商量、就這麼定了、不用再說了（也可以說 that's final）

I'm not coming with you, and <u>that's flat</u>!

我不會跟你們去的，不用再說了！

7. 「一段短時間＋ **flat**」指一件事情發生僅僅需要所述的時間

This car will move you from 0 to 60mph in <u>three seconds flat</u>.

這輛車從時速 0 到 60 英里只需 3 秒。

Fresh

新的；無經驗的；無禮的、輕佻放肆的；精力充沛的

▶ MP3-059

fresh approach　新的方法

With the government's failure to solve the problem of unemployment, a <u>fresh approach</u> is necessary.
由於政府未能處理好失業問題，我們有必要採取新的方法。

fresh evidence　新的證據

<u>Fresh evidence</u> has emerged that casts doubt on the man's conviction.
新的證據浮上檯面，也使男子的判決受到質疑。

fresh idea　新的想法

These interior designers are full of <u>fresh ideas</u>.
這些室內設計師滿腦子都是新點子。

fresh impetus　新的動力

The present conflict may provide <u>fresh impetus</u> for peace talks.
目前的衝突可能會為和平談判帶來新的動力。

fresh insight 新的見解

Her book offers some <u>fresh insights</u> into the events leading up to the war.
她的書針對導致那場戰爭的事件提出新見解。

fresh look 重新審視、看待

We need to take a <u>fresh look</u> at the problem.
我們必須重新看待這個問題。

fresh perspective 新的觀點

He recommended me to look at the issue with a <u>fresh perspective</u>.
他建議我用新的觀點來看這個議題。

fresh start 新的開始

Her divorce gave her an opportunity to make a <u>fresh start</u>.
離婚讓她有機會重新開始。

fresh thinking 新的思維

Even a failure can prompt <u>fresh thinking</u> and changes.
即使是失敗，也能激發新的思維和改變。

fresh blood 新血、新成員（也可以說 new blood）

The company has brought in some <u>fresh blood</u> in an effort to revive its fortunes.

公司招募了一些新血，打算藉此重振雄風。

實用短語 / 用法 / 句型　　▶ MP3-060

1. **to be fresh from / out of sth** 剛從～出來的

   There's nothing better than the bread <u>fresh from</u> the oven.

   沒有什麼比剛出爐的麵包更好的了。

   That is an important group interview for this guy <u>fresh out of</u> university.

   對於這個剛從大學畢業的社會新鮮人來說，那是一場重要的團體面試。

2. **to be fresh in sb's memory / mind** 記憶猶新

   I'd like to take the test soon, while the information is still <u>fresh in my mind</u>.

   趁我還記得資料的時候，我想快點考試。

3. **to get fresh with sb** 對某人輕佻放肆

   A man <u>got fresh with</u> her in the bar, so she slapped his face.

   一個男人在酒吧裡對她毛手毛腳，所以她賞了對方耳光。

4. **(as) fresh as a daisy** 精力充沛的

   After a good night's sleep, I'll be <u>as fresh as a daisy</u>.

   好好睡一覺，我就會精力充沛。

Genuine 真正的；真誠的、真心的 ▶ MP3-061

genuine article 真品

Some fake designer clothes are so good that people have no idea they're not buying the genuine articles.
有些冒牌服飾做得太像，民眾完全不知道自己買的不是真品。

genuine leather 真皮

The brown dress shoes made of genuine leather on the shelf aroused our attention.
架上的真皮褐色皮鞋引起了我們的注意。

genuine affection 真誠的情感

The photographer will be remembered with genuine affection.
人們將真心銘記這位攝影師。

genuine appreciation 真摯的感謝

I would like to express my genuine appreciation for all the work you have done.
我想對你們所做的一切表達真心的感謝。

genuine attempt 真心的嘗試

This is the first genuine attempt to reach a peaceful settlement to the dispute.
這是第一次真的嘗試要和平解決爭端。

genuine compassion / concern 真誠的同情 / 關心

The reforms are motivated by a genuine concern for the disabled.
改革的動機來自於對殘疾人士真誠的關心。

genuine desire 真正的心願

His genuine desire to compensate her may be interpreted as an intrigue.
他真正想要補償她的想法可能被解讀為是某種計謀。

genuine interest 真心的興趣

The meeting is open to all with a genuine interest in having a say in the future of their community.
這次會議是完全開放的，所有有興趣替社區未來發聲的人都能參與。

genuine opinion 真誠的想法

In an emotional moment, the operating officer let her genuine opinions be known.
在感性的時刻，營運長透露了她真誠的想法。

genuine pleasure 真正的快樂

It was a <u>genuine pleasure</u> to do an interview with a master talking about his work.

能和大師談論他的工作是件非常愉快的事。

genuine regret / remorse 真心的後悔 / 自責

The defendant lied to the police, lied to the court and demonstrated little <u>genuine remorse</u>.

被告對警方和法庭撒謊，沒有一絲懊悔。

genuine surprise 真心的驚訝

He was in <u>genuine surprise</u> when she suddenly appeared at the airport.

她突然出現在機場，他感到非常驚訝。

Hard

困難的、艱難的；堅硬的；努力的、勤奮的；
用力的；嚴格的、冷酷無情的；嚴寒的；確實的、
不容懷疑的；烈的

▶ MP3-062

hard day / time 艱辛、忙碌的日子

I am really tired after a <u>hard day</u> at work.
工作忙了一天，我真的累壞了。

hard going 難進行的過程、困境

The book runs to some 1,200 pages and I found it rather
<u>hard going</u>.
這本書多達 1,200 頁，我覺得它很難懂。

hard luck 倒楣、不幸

I have been having a lot of <u>hard luck</u> lately. It seems like
nothing is going right for me!
我最近很倒楣，似乎沒一件事是順利的！

hard news 重大新聞

TV news programs nowadays seem to be more interested
in gossip than in <u>hard news</u>.
現在的電視新聞似乎對八卦比較有興趣，而不是重大新聞。

hard feelings 反感、怒氣

She insisted she has no hard feelings toward her partner.
她堅持說自己對夥伴沒有怨氣。

hard line 強硬路線、強硬立場

The school takes a very hard line on drugs.
這所學校對毒品的態度非常強硬。

hard words 難聽的言詞、罵人的話

Don't utter hard words even if you feel angry.
即使生氣你也不要說難聽的話。

hard winter 寒冬

In a hard winter, wild animals can die from food shortages.
寒冬時，野生動物可能因為缺乏食物而死亡。

hard evidence / fact / information
鐵證 / 不可動搖的事實 / 確切的資訊

No one has hard evidence to back up his or her argument.
沒人有確切的證據支持自己的論點。

hard liquor 烈酒

Most doctors recommend cutting back on hard liquor.
大部分的醫生都建議少喝烈酒。

1.　**to be hard at it / work** 努力做某事

He <u>is hard at work</u> on the translation of a play that has to be ready in two days.
他正在努力翻譯一齣兩天後要完成的劇本。

2.　**to be hard on sb** 對某人嚴苛

He is a severe-looking man, who is known to <u>be hard on</u> students.
他外表嚴肅，對學生出了名的嚴格。

3.　**to be hard put to do sth** 難以做某事

You <u>are hard put to</u> make intimate friends in the competitive business world.
在競爭激烈的商場上，你很難交到知心朋友。

4.　**to be hard up** 缺錢

We <u>are</u> a bit <u>hard up</u> at the moment so we're not thinking about holidays.
我們現在手頭有點緊，所以沒有考慮去度假。

5.　**to drive / strike a hard bargain** 討價還價

The bank is able to <u>drive a hard bargain</u> because the company badly needs cash.
因為公司急需現金，銀行可以和它討價還價。

6.　**to fall on hard times** 窮困潦倒、陷入困境

The scheme is designed to help kids whose parents have <u>fallen on hard times</u>.
這個計畫的目的，是幫助那些父母陷入經濟困境的孩子。

7. to give sb a hard time 為難某人

The man decided to tender his resignation because his boss was <u>giving</u> him <u>a</u> really <u>hard time</u>.

因為老闆為難他，他決定辭職。

8. to go hard with sb 使某人遭遇麻煩、困難、痛苦

The police will <u>go hard with</u> you if you don't tell the truth.

如果你不說實話，警察會找你麻煩。

9. to have a hard time 遇到困難或者不好的經驗

I <u>had a hard time</u> persuading them to accept the offer.

我費盡千辛萬苦說服他們接受這個提議。

10. to learn sth the hard way

吃盡苦頭、費了一番功夫才學會、理解

He <u>learned the hard way</u> about the harsh reality of the business world.

他吃盡了苦頭才了解商場上殘酷的現實。

11. to make hard work of sth 將簡單的事情變複雜

You can <u>make hard work of</u> an easy job if you don't know the right way to go.

如果不知道對的方法，你會把一件簡單的工作搞得很複雜。

12. to play hard to get

欲擒故縱、故作冷淡、裝作對某人不感興趣

We know that the girl is just <u>playing hard to get</u>.
我們都知道那女孩只是故作冷淡。

13. to take a (long) hard look at sb / sth

仔細思考～、認真審視～

The U.S. government needs to <u>take a long, hard look at</u> gun control.
美國政府必須認真審視槍枝管制的問題。

14. (as) hard as a rock / stone 像石頭一樣硬的

This French bread is <u>as hard as a rock</u>.
這法國麵包硬得跟石頭一樣。

15. hard and fast 嚴格的、不容改變的

There are no <u>hard and fast</u> rules about when you should show up at the office.
公司沒有硬性規定你幾點要到班。

16. hard-hearted 鐵石心腸的、冷酷無情的

If you don't know him well, you might think he is a <u>hard-hearted</u> and cruel man.
你如果跟他不熟的話，你可能會覺得他冷酷無情。

17. too much like hard work

某人覺得某事太辛苦，而不願去做

Becoming a doctor never interested him. It was <u>too much like hard work</u> for him.
他從來對當醫生不感興趣，因為那太辛苦了。

Harsh 嚴厲的；惡劣的、艱苦的；刺眼的、刺耳的

harsh criticism / word 嚴厲的批評 / 難聽的話

The proposal is open to harsh criticism.
這項提案受到嚴厲的批評。

harsh discipline 嚴厲的紀律

This private school is known for its harsh discipline.
這所私立學校以其嚴格的紀律聞名。

harsh penalty / punishment / treatment

嚴厲的處罰 / 對待

The teacher has been criticized for his harsh treatment of his students.
這位老師因為對學生的管教嚴格而受到批評。

harsh tone / voice 嚴厲的口氣

"There is no alternative," he said in a harsh voice.
他嚴厲地說：「沒有選擇的餘地。」

harsh climate / weather / winter 惡劣的氣候 / 天氣 / 寒冬

The weather is growing harsh, chilly and unpredictable.
天氣變得越來越惡劣、寒冷、不可預測。

harsh condition / environment 嚴苛的條件、惡劣的環境

The hostages are being held in <u>harsh conditions</u>.
人質處於惡劣的環境中。

harsh reality / truth 殘酷的現實／事實

The book confronts the <u>harsh</u> social and political <u>realities</u> of the world today.
這本書赤裸裸地探討了現今社會與政治的殘酷現實。

harsh terrain 嚴苛的地形

The nomadic people have to trek across the <u>harsh terrain</u>.
遊牧民族必須穿越這嚴苛的地形。

harsh glare / lighting / sunlight 刺眼的光線

I personally prefer candles to the <u>harsh glare</u> of electric lighting.
我個人比較喜歡蠟燭，不喜歡電燈刺眼的光線。

Hasty 匆忙的；倉促的、草率的

▶ MP3-065

hasty departure / exit 匆忙離開

He fielded a number of questions from the audience before he made a hasty exit.
他在匆忙離開前回答了一些觀眾的問題。

hasty meal 匆忙的一餐、匆忙吃完飯

After the hasty meal, employees moved forward to take up their positions.
匆忙吃完飯後，員工繼續工作。

hasty retreat 匆忙撤退

We were forced to beat a hasty retreat and arrived at our rendezvous before dawn.
我們被迫匆忙撤退，在黎明前抵達會合點。

We saw the rain and made a hasty retreat into a convenience store.
我們看到下雨就連忙躲進便利商店。

hasty conclusion 草率的結論

We should not jump to the wrong, hasty conclusion before the project is carried out.
在計畫執行前，我們不應該做出草率、錯誤的結論。

hasty decision 倉促的決定

A number of friends urged him not to make a <u>hasty decision</u>.
一些朋友勸他不要倉促做決定。

Heartfelt 衷心的、真誠的

▶ MP3-066

heartfelt apology 衷心的道歉

We offered her a heartfelt apology and a bunch of flowers.
我們對她表達衷心的歉意並送上一束花。

heartfelt appreciation / thanks 由衷的感謝

The winner expressed her heartfelt thanks to all those who had helped and supported her.
得獎人對所有曾經幫助及支持她的人表達由衷的感謝。

heartfelt desire / wish 衷心的希望 / 祝福

Our most heartfelt wish is for our children to be happy.
我們衷心希望小孩能開心。

heartfelt emotion / sentiment 真誠的情感、感受

The director is trying to do away with the sneers and make a genuine film with heartfelt emotions.
導演試圖擺脫那些嘲笑，用真摯的情感做出一部真正的好電影。

heartfelt plea 衷心的請求

The family made a heartfelt plea to the kidnappers to release their son.
家人衷心請求綁匪放了他們的兒子。

heartfelt sympathy 發自內心的同情

Our <u>heartfelt sympathy</u> goes out to him and his wife.
我們發自內心同情他和他太太。

Hearty

衷心的、熱情的；大量的、豐盛的；盡情的；健壯的

▶ MP3-067

hearty approval / congratulations / thanks

衷心的贊同 / 祝賀 / 感謝

Please accept my hearty congratulations.
請接受我衷心的祝賀。

hearty cheer / welcome　熱情的歡呼 / 歡迎

The audience gave us all a hearty welcome.
觀眾熱情歡迎我們。

hearty endorsement　衷心的支持

His new design won hearty endorsement from the head office.
他的新設計贏得了總部的衷心支持。

hearty handshake　熱情的握手

He received many cheerful greetings and a hearty handshake from the leader of the team.
他受到了熱烈歡呼，隊長也上前和他熱情地握手。

hearty appetite / eater 胃口很好 / 食量很大的人

We went for a walk to work up a <u>hearty appetite</u> for dinner.
我們去散步了一下，好讓晚餐的時候更有食慾。

hearty food / meal 豐盛的食物 / 一餐

We enjoyed a <u>hearty meal</u> before we set off.
我們出發前吃了豐盛的一餐。

hearty laugh 大笑、開懷大笑

We all had a <u>hearty laugh</u> about that afterwards.
我們後來都對那件事開懷大笑。

實用短語 / 用法 / 句型　　▶ MP3-068

1. **hale and hearty** 老當益壯的
   My grandfather is <u>hale and hearty</u>, walking five kilometers each day before breakfast.
   我爺爺老當益壯，他每天早餐前都會走個 5 公里。

Heated 激烈的、憤怒的

▶ MP3-069

heated argument / debate / discussion

激烈的爭論 / 辯論 / 討論

The gun control issue continues to be the subject of <u>heated debate</u>.

槍枝管制一直都是激烈辯論的話題。

heated controversy 激烈的爭議

The policy has caused <u>heated controversy</u> ever since it was introduced.

自從推行以來，這項政策已經引起激烈的爭議。

heated conversation / exchange 激動的談話

Two managers had a <u>heated exchange</u> in the meeting.

兩位經理在會議上的對談相當激動。

Heavy

重的、厚重的；繁重的、費力的；劇烈的、大量的；（心情）沉重的；（食物）難消化的；（情況）嚴重的、麻煩的

▶ MP3-070

heavy breathing 大聲、沉重的呼吸

The locker room is full of <u>heavy breathing</u> and the stink of our sweat.
更衣室充滿沉重的呼吸聲和我們的汗臭味。

heavy perfume / scent 重的、濃的氣味

The <u>heavy perfume</u> hit me as I walked by the lady.
我從那女士身旁走過，聞到很重的香水味。

heavy burden / load / responsibility 重擔、重責

Many staff members complained about the <u>heavy</u> administrative <u>burden</u>.
很多員工抱怨沉重的行政負擔。

heavy date 重要的約會（美、澳）

I guess William has a <u>heavy date</u>—he has been doing his hair for over thirty minutes.
威廉已經整理頭髮超過半小時了，我猜他有重要的約會。

heavy traffic 繁忙的交通

We were slightly late because the <u>heavy traffic</u> detained us for almost an hour.
交通壅塞耽擱了我們將近 1 個小時，導致我們有點遲到。

heavy work / workload 繁重的工作 / 工作量

We sent a couple of seasoned employees to do the <u>heavy work</u>.
我們派了幾個經驗豐富的員工來負責這項繁重的工作。

heavy casualties / losses 傷亡 / 損失慘重

Taliban militants have inflicted <u>heavy casualties</u> on civilian populations in Pakistan.
塔利班激進份子已經造成巴基斯坦人民重大死傷。

heavy defeat 慘敗

We suffered a <u>heavy defeat</u> because we did not play well in the final game.
因為在最後一場比賽中表現失常，我們遭遇慘敗。

heavy downpour / rain / snow / thunderstorm
大雨 / 大雪 / 大雷雨

The water level in the reservoir rose up during the <u>heavy downpours</u>.
水庫水位在暴雨期間上升。

heavy drinker / smoker 酒癮 / 菸癮很重的人

Her husband was a <u>heavy smoker</u> who died of lung cancer.
她老公的菸癮很重,死於肺癌。

heavy emphasis 非常強調

To my mind, many schools in Taiwan do not put a <u>heavy emphasis</u> on sporting achievements.
我認為許多台灣學校不重視體育成就。

heavy fighting 激戰

<u>Heavy fighting</u> took place near the border between Iraq and Syria.
伊拉克和敍利亞邊界爆發激烈戰爭。

heavy fine / price 巨額罰款

The popular restaurant was hit by a <u>heavy fine</u> after mice were found in the kitchen.
那間知名餐廳被直擊廚房有老鼠後,被處以巨額罰款。

heavy price 沉重的代價

The team paid a <u>heavy price</u> for its lack of preparation.
這支隊伍為準備不足付出了沉重的代價。

heavy reliance 大量依賴

A <u>heavy reliance</u> on a particular market may be dangerous for companies.
過度依賴單一特定市場對公司可能很危險。

heavy sleeper 睡得很熟、很難叫醒的人

I'm such a <u>heavy sleeper</u> that his snores didn't wake me.
我睡得很熟,他的打鼾聲並沒有把我吵醒。

heavy use 大量使用

Without the <u>heavy use</u> of fertilizers, there would be no crops for us.
要是不大量使用肥料,我們就會沒有收穫。

heavy heart 沉重的心情

He handed over his resignation letter with a <u>heavy heart</u>.
他沉重地遞交辭呈。

heavy meal 難消化的大餐

He has been feeling drowsy since he ate a <u>heavy meal</u>.
吃完大餐之後,他一直昏昏欲睡。

1.　to be / get heavy with / on sb 對某人嚴厲

My parents are <u>getting heavy with</u> me in terms of schoolwork.
在課業方面，爸媽對我越來越嚴厲。

2.　to be heavy on sth 大量使用、消耗（英）

This car <u>is heavy on</u> oil. 這輛車很耗油。

3.　to make heavy weather of sth
把某事搞得很複雜（貶義）（英）

He's <u>making</u> such <u>heavy weather of</u> the project that he is doing.
他把企劃搞得很複雜。

4.　to take a heavy toll on sth / sb
造成嚴重的負面影響

The recession has <u>taken a heavy toll on</u> many of our retail stores.
這波經濟衰退潮重創我們的零售店。

5.　heavy going 很難理解或是很無趣的書或事

I like the film but, to be honest, the novel is rather <u>heavy going</u>.
我喜歡這部電影，但老實說，它的小說很難懂。

Hectic 忙碌的、繁忙的

▶ MP3-072

hectic day / life 忙碌的日子、生活

Failing to return calls and reply to emails are common omissions during <u>hectic days</u> at work.
在工作繁忙的日子裡，忘記回覆電話和郵件是常有的事。

hectic pace 忙碌的步調

Boracay has become a paradise for people tired of the <u>hectic pace</u> of city life.
對厭倦繁忙生活步調的都市人來說，菲律賓長灘島已經成為了他們的度假天堂。

hectic schedule 緊湊的行程

Despite his <u>hectic</u> work <u>schedule</u>, the man has rarely suffered from poor health.
儘管工作行程很緊湊，他的身體卻很少出狀況。

Hidden 隱藏的

▶ MP3-073

hidden agenda / motive 隱藏的意圖、動機

The government has denied that there is any <u>hidden agenda</u> behind the plan.
政府否認這個計畫背後有任何隱藏的企圖。

hidden charges / costs / expenses / extras
隱藏的額外費用

Consumers need more protection against <u>hidden charges</u> often tucked away in the fine print.
消費者需要更多的保障，防止他們被收取隱藏在附屬條約裡的額外費用。

hidden danger / menace 隱藏的危險、威脅

The author hopes, through this article, that more people will have the awareness of the <u>hidden dangers</u> of fast food.
作者希望透過這篇文章，讓更多人意識到速食的潛在危險。

hidden flaw 隱藏的缺點

There is a <u>hidden flaw</u> in the structure's design.
這棟建築的設計有個隱藏缺點。

hidden gem　隱藏的好地方、隱藏的美好事物、私房景點

There are many <u>hidden gems</u> in the city just waiting to be discovered.
城市裡有很多私房景點等待被發掘。

hidden meaning / message　隱藏的意義 / 訊息

There are quite a few <u>hidden messages</u> in this movie.
這部電影暗藏很多訊息。

hidden secret / truth　隱藏的祕密 / 真相

The defector has a lot of dark, <u>hidden secrets</u> in her young life.
這個逃亡者的幼年生活有許多不可告人的祕密。

hidden talent　潛在的才能

The teacher wants each student to have the chance to discover <u>hidden talents</u>.
老師想讓每個學生都有機會發掘自己的潛能。

hidden treasure　隱藏的寶藏

Grave robbers hunt for <u>hidden treasure</u> at the risk of their lives.
盜墓者冒著生命危險找尋隱藏的寶藏。

hidden value 潛在的價值

The documentary raises awareness among the audience of the <u>hidden values</u> of biodiversity.

這部紀錄片喚起觀眾的意識，讓他們察覺到生物多樣性的潛在價值。

High

高的；（地位、程度）高的、重要的；情緒高昂的、正盛的；含量高的

▶ MP3-074

high achiever 有高成就的人、表現優異的人

Although he came from a humble background, he was a high achiever.
他雖然出身卑微，卻成就不凡。

high alert 高度警戒

Early in the war, troops were put on high alert.
戰爭初期，軍隊處於高度警戒狀態。

high caliber / quality / standard 高品質、高水準

This restaurant strives to maintain the highest quality of service.
這間餐廳力求維持最高品質的服務。

high casualties 傷亡慘重（也可以說 heavy casualties）

The terrorist attack in London resulted in high casualties.
發生在倫敦的恐怖攻擊造成嚴重傷亡。

high esteem / regard 高度敬重、非常尊敬

In the United States, university professors are held in high esteem.
大學教授在美國受到高度敬重。

high expectations / hopes 高期望

We have <u>high expectations</u> of winning first prize in the match.
我們對贏得第一名抱持很大的期望。

high importance / priority 非常重要

Luxuries are not a <u>high priority</u> for me.
奢侈品對我來說不是很重要。

high prevalence 高度流行

There is <u>high prevalence</u> of malaria in the tropics.
瘧疾在熱帶地區高度流行。

high opinion / praise / reputation 評價很高、好評、盛譽

The watch brand won <u>high opinions</u> from teenagers soon after it hit the market.
這個手錶品牌一上市，就獲得年輕人的好評。

high percentage / proportion 比例很高

A <u>high proportion</u> of women with children under five work full-time.
有 5 歲以下小孩的女性中，很大一部分都是全職媽媽。

high position / rank / status 高地位、重要的位置

Such clothes were expensive at that time and were a symbol of high status.
這樣的服飾在當時非常昂貴，是重要地位的象徵。

high profile 高姿態、高調

They seek neither the spotlight nor the high-profile social life.
他們不追求鎂光燈、也不追求高調的社交生活。

high society 上流社會

French was considered the language of refinement and high society through the 19th century.
19 世紀時，法語被認為是優雅、上流社會的語言。

high noon / summer 正中午 / 盛夏

In order to buy the latest iPhone 10, people were willing to line up in front of the store at high noon.
為了買到最新的 iPhone 10，民眾正中午也願意在店門口排隊。

high point / spot （活動、期間的）亮點、高潮

The visit to the ancient capital city was one of the high spots of the tour.
參觀古老首都是這趟旅行的亮點之一。

high season　旺季

People on a tight budget should avoid traveling during the high season.
預算有限的民眾應該避免在旺季旅遊。

high spirits　情緒高昂、興奮的狀態

They'd had a couple of drinks and were in high spirits.
他們喝了幾杯酒，聊得正高興。

實用短語 / 用法 / 句型　　▶ MP3-075

1. **to be / get on one's high horse**
   目空一切、自認為比別人好
   You should not get on your high horse and judge others' opinions.
   你不應該自以為是地評斷別人的意見。

2. **to begin / end / finish on a high note**
   完美成功地開始 / 結束
   The concert ended on a high note last night.
   昨晚的演唱會完美落幕。

3. **to be high in sth**　富含～
   My doctor asked me to avoid fried food because it is high in fat.
   醫生要我少吃油炸食物，因為它的脂肪含量很高。

4. to be high on the agenda / list (of priorities)
首要之務

The rights of minorities will <u>be high on the agenda</u>
at the conference.
少數族群的權益將會是這場會議的首要之務。

5. to be high up in sth 在～的地位、位階很高

Her husband <u>is high up in</u> the navy.
她老公在海軍裡的位階很高。

6. to run high （情緒）高漲

Emotions <u>ran high</u> throughout the final game on
Friday night.
週五晚上的決賽中，觀眾的情緒高漲。

7. high and dry 面臨困難卻沒人給予幫助

It seems that I've been left <u>high and dry</u> and have
to do all the work by myself.
看來似乎沒辦法得到幫助了，所有工作必須由我自己來
做。

8. high and mighty 趾高氣昂的、盛氣凌人的（反諷語氣）

He has been acting all <u>high and mighty</u> since he
got his promotion.
升遷後，他就一副趾高氣昂的樣子。

9. high days and holidays 節慶假日

This dish was traditionally made only on <u>high days
and holidays</u>.
這道菜傳統上只有在節慶假日才吃得到。

10. it is high time 該是～的時候了

<u>It is high time</u> that we stood up for same-sex marriage.

該是我們站出來支持同性婚姻的時候了。

Inclement （天氣）惡劣的、嚴酷的

inclement weather 惡劣的天氣

Many flights are postponed due to <u>inclement weather</u>.
由於天氣惡劣，許多航班延誤。

In the event of <u>inclement weather</u>, the ceremony would be held indoors.
在天氣惡劣的狀況下，我們將在室內舉行典禮。

Instant 立即的；緊急的、迫切的

▶ MP3-077

instant access 立即使用、立即取得

The service is designed to provide <u>instant access</u> to colleagues who have similar problems.
這項服務的目的，是讓我們能即時和有類似問題的同事取得聯繫。

instant answer / reply / response 立即回覆

We got an <u>instant response</u> from the travel agency.
我們馬上就收到旅行社的回覆。

instant result / solution 立即的結果 / 解決方法

The manager will have to take control over the project and come up with an <u>instant solution</u>.
經理將必須接管這個計畫，想出一個立即的解決方案。

instant bestseller / classic / fame / hit / success

爆紅、一夕成名（也可以說 overnight sensation，不過 instant bestseller / classic 大多用來形容作品）

The book became an <u>instant hit</u> after many celebrities bought it.
許多名人買了這本書之後，它就一夕爆紅。

Contrary to public expectations, the film was an <u>instant success</u>.
與大眾預期相反，這部電影一上映就大獲好評。

instant coffee 即溶咖啡

When you are almost late for work, <u>instant coffee</u> is a good option for you.
當你上班快遲到時，即溶咖啡是個好選擇。

instant communication / message 即時通訊

If you receive emails or <u>instant messages</u> that upset you, just try to ignore them.
如果你收到煩人的郵件或訊息，就試著忽略它們。

instant confirmation 立即確認

Online reservation is also available, and you will receive <u>instant confirmation</u>.
您也可以線上訂房，立即收到預訂確認。

instant dislike / liking 立刻、第一眼就不喜歡 / 喜歡

When the two men met, they took an <u>instant dislike</u> to each other.
這兩個男人一見面就不喜歡對方。

instant feedback 即時回饋

In this class, you will be able to receive <u>instant feedback</u> from instructors.
在這堂課當中，你將能夠從講師們那得到即時的回饋。

instant gratification 即時滿足

Most people have been trained to expect <u>instant gratification</u> these days.

如今，多數人都已經習慣預期自己的需求能被即時滿足。

instant information / notification 即時的資訊 / 通知

They failed to give <u>instant notification</u> of their intention to demolish the building.

他們沒有立即通知住戶大樓將被拆除。

instant noodles 速食麵、泡麵

<u>Instant noodles</u> are a must for those who are going to travel abroad.

泡麵是出國旅行的必備品。

instant help 即時的幫助、緊急救助

It is the responsibility of the government to provide the typhoon victims with <u>instant help</u>.

提供颱風受災者緊急救助是政府的職責。

Intense 強烈的、劇烈的、熱烈的

▶ MP3-078

intense activity 熱烈的活動

The opening of the stadium will be preceded by an <u>intense activity</u>.
在體育館的開幕式前會先有熱烈的活動。

intense anger / anguish 極度憤怒 / 痛苦

The man's words stirred up other passengers' <u>intense anger</u>.
這人的話激起了其他乘客的強烈憤怒。

intense fighting 激戰

At least 1,000 people have been killed in a week of <u>intense fighting</u> in Iraq.
伊拉克激戰中，一週內已經至少有 1,000 人喪生。

intense competition / rivalry 激烈的競爭

<u>Intense competition</u> ensures that only a few actors secure the contract.
激烈的競爭確保只有少數演員能獲得合約。

intense concentration 高度的專注

Being a pilot is a job that demands <u>intense concentration</u>.
機師是一份需要高度專注的工作。

intense debate / negotiations 激烈的爭論 / 協商

There has been (an) <u>intense debate</u> about whether abortion should be allowed.
關於墮胎是否該被允許，一直有激烈的爭論。

intense dislike / hatred 強烈的厭惡、痛恨

Several committee members expressed their <u>intense dislike</u> of the chairman.
幾名委員會的成員表達了他們對主席的強烈不滿。

intense feeling / emotion 強烈的情感、情緒

Don't feel embarrassed about crying, as you will feel better after you release these <u>intense emotions</u>.
不用覺得哭很尷尬，因為在你釋放這些強烈的情緒後，你會感覺好一些。

intense interest 強烈的、濃厚的興趣

She takes an <u>intense interest</u> in international relations.
她對國際關係有強烈的興趣。

intense pain 劇痛

She suddenly felt an <u>intense pain</u> in her back.
她突然覺得背部一陣劇痛。

intense pressure 極大的壓力

Young people nowadays are under <u>intense pressure</u> to succeed.
現代年輕人為了成功承受了極大的壓力。

intense scrutiny 嚴格的檢查

The company has come under <u>intense scrutiny</u> because of its environmental record.
因為環保紀錄的關係，公司受到嚴格檢查。

intense speculation 諸多的猜測

After weeks of <u>intense speculation</u>, the actor and the actress eventually announced that they were going to get married.
幾週來的諸多猜測後，這兩位演員終於宣布他們要結婚了。

Keen
熱切的、渴望的；強烈的、激烈的；敏銳的、銳利的

▶ MP3-079

keen anticipation 熱切的期望

I cannot deny my keen anticipation of his visit.
我不能否認我熱切期待他的來訪。

keen supporter 熱衷的支持者

He's been a keen supporter of the team all his life.
他一生都是這個隊伍的死忠支持者。

keen competition 激烈的競爭

They won the contest in the face of keen competition.
他們在激烈競爭中贏得了比賽。

keen interest 強烈的興趣

He takes a keen interest in politics and foreign affairs.
他對政治和外交有強烈的興趣。

keen price 低價

The company negotiated very keen prices with its suppliers.
公司和供應商討論後取得超低的價格。

a keen sense of sth 強烈的～感

He is a man with a keen sense of public duty.
他有強烈的公共責任感。

keen appreciation 敏銳的鑑賞力

The course helped me to gain a keen appreciation of
movies.
這門課使我對電影有了敏銳的鑑賞力。

keen awareness 高度的意識、敏銳性

Keen awareness of the similarities and differences between
the two languages can facilitate learning.
對兩種語言之間的異同有高度的意識能幫助學習。

keen eye 銳利的眼光

She has a keen eye for talent.
她對人才有銳利的眼光。

keen insight / intellect / mind / wit
敏銳的見解 / 才智 / 思維 / 機智

With her keen mind and good business sense, she soon
became noticed.
有著敏銳的思維和優秀的商業頭腦，她很快就被注意到。

實用短語 / 用法 / 句型　▶ MP3-080

1. **to be keen on sb / sth** 對～感興趣；迷上某人

   Both companies <u>are keen on</u> a merger.

   兩家公司都對合併有興趣。

2. **to be mad keen on sth** 對～非常著迷

   The kids <u>are mad keen on</u> computer games at the moment.

   小孩現在非常著迷於電腦遊戲。

3. **(as) keen as mustard** 很感興趣、極為熱切

   I gave him the job because he was willing to learn and seemed <u>as keen as mustard</u>.

   因為他願意學習又很有熱誠，所以我給了他這份工作。

Large 大的;大量的;大規模的

large amount / number

大量（amount 修飾不可數名詞；number 修飾可數名詞）

We have made good progress, but there is still a <u>large amount</u> of work to be done.
我們已經有很大的進展了，但仍有相當多的工作要做。

So far a <u>large number</u> of students have signed up for the course.
目前已經有很多學生報名這門課程。

large fortune 大筆財產

He inherited a <u>large fortune</u> from his father, but soon gambled it all away.
他繼承父親的大筆財產，但很快就賭光了。

large population 大量的人口

China nowadays has the <u>largest population</u> in the world.
中國現在擁有世界上最多的人口。

large company / organization 大規模的公司 / 組織

When you are young, working for a <u>large company</u> will be better because you can learn a lot.
年輕的時候，在大公司上班比較好，因為你能學到很多東西。

large scale 大規模

We must improve our response to <u>large-scale</u> natural disasters.
我們必須提高對大規模自然災害的反應能力。

實用短語 / 用法 / 句型　　▶ MP3-082

1. **to loom large** 顯得格外重要
   The issue of the global financial crisis will <u>loom large</u> at this year's conference.
   全球金融危機的議題在今年的會議上顯得格外重要。

2. **(as) large as life** 本人（表示驚訝）
   I looked up from my novel and there she was, <u>as large as life</u>, Emma Watson!
   我看小說看到一半抬起頭來，竟然遇見艾瑪華森本人！

3. **at large** 自由的、未束縛住的
   Those who robbed the bank are still <u>at large</u>.
   銀行搶匪還在逃。

4. **by and large** 整體而言、大致上
   Although I cannot totally accept your point, I think <u>by and large</u> it is reasonable.
   雖然我不能完全同意你的看法，但它大致上是合理的。

5. **in large measure / part** 很大的程度上、大部分
   The success of today's conference was due <u>in large measure</u> to its organizers.
   今天會議能成功，大部分都要歸功於籌備人。

6. larger than life 意義非凡的；有趣的；活躍的

The public love Mr. Lin a lot, who is <u>larger than life</u> and always exudes a sense of fun.

群眾都很喜歡林先生，因為他總是很活潑有趣。

Lenient 仁慈的、寬厚的

▶ MP3-083

lenient sentence 仁慈的判決、輕判

The previous <u>lenient sentence</u> for drunk driving has proven ineffective, as drivers will often take the chance, believing they will not be caught.
先前對酒駕從輕判決證明沒有效用，因為駕駛人經常會心存僥倖，覺得自己不會被抓到。

lenient treatment 仁慈的對待、寬容的處理

The criminals surrendered themselves to the police, hoping to receive <u>lenient treatment</u> from the government.
犯人向警方自首，希望政府能從輕量刑。

lenient view 寬容的觀點

The professor took a <u>lenient view</u> of the case.
教授對這案子持寬容的態度。

實用短語 / 用法 / 句型　　▶ MP3-084

1. **to be lenient with sb** 對某人仁慈
   They believe that judges <u>are</u> too <u>lenient with</u> drug dealers.
   他們認為法官對毒販太過仁慈。

Liberal 開明的；自由的、開放的；慷慨的、大方的；大量的；模糊的、籠統的 ▶ MP3-085

liberal attitude / view 開明的態度

Nowadays, teenagers take a more <u>liberal attitude</u> toward sex.
現在年輕人對性的態度比較開放。

liberal democracy 自由民主的國家

This country is a <u>liberal democracy</u> with a multiparty system.
這是一個多黨制的自由民主國家。

liberal policy 開放的政策

The candidate has promised more <u>liberal</u> economic <u>policies</u> if he is elected.
這個候選人承諾，如果他當選的話，將會推動更開放的經濟政策。

liberal society 自由民主的社會

Everyone's opinions should be respected in a <u>liberal society</u>.
在自由民主的社會，每個人的意見都該受到尊重。

liberal amount / supply 大量 / 大量供應

There was a <u>liberal supply</u> of food and wine at the party.
這次派對提供了大量的食物和酒。

liberal use 大量使用

The paper makes <u>liberal use</u> of the notion brought forth in 1995.
這篇論文大量使用 1995 年所提出的一個概念。

liberal education 通才教育

Many scholars advocate <u>liberal education</u> in university.
許多學者提倡在大學實行通才教育。

liberal interpretation 籠統的解釋

To avoid upsetting previous judgments, the court used a <u>liberal interpretation</u> of the law.
為了避免推翻先前的判決，法庭採用了該法條的籠統解釋。

實用短語 / 用法 / 句型　　▶ MP3-086

1. **to be liberal with** 對～慷慨
   The successful entrepreneur <u>is</u> quite <u>liberal with</u> his cash.
   這位成功的企業家出手很大方。

Light 輕的；明亮的、淺色的；少量的、輕微的；輕鬆的、輕快的

▶ MP3-087

light drinker / eater / smoker

不太喝酒 / 食量不大 / 菸癮不大的人

I'm a light drinker, only drinking on special days.
我不太喝酒，只有在特別的日子會喝。

light lunch / meal 輕食

A light meal usually contains salad, sandwiches, and bread.
輕食通常包含沙拉、三明治和麵包。

light rain 小雨

Saturday will be a cloudy day with outbreaks of mainly light rain in western areas.
週六會是多雲的天氣，西部地區帶有突發性小雨。

light sentence 輕的判刑

She got off with a fairly light sentence because it was her first conviction.
因為這是她第一次被定罪，所以只受到相當輕的刑罰。

light sleeper 容易被吵醒的人、淺眠的人

He's a light sleeper—the slightest noise wakes him.
他很淺眠，再小的聲音都可以吵醒他。

light heart 輕鬆的心情

Knowing that he would be promoted, he went back to his office with a light heart.
得知自己將要升遷，他輕鬆愉快地回到辦公室。

light reading 休閒的讀物

That's a really good book if you want a bit of light reading.
如果你想要讀點輕鬆的東西，那會是一本很棒的書。

light relief 讓人感到輕鬆的東西

A heated argument between the two main speakers provided some light relief in a dull meeting.
兩個主講人間激烈的爭辯讓無聊的會議稍稍有趣一點。

light work 輕鬆的、負擔不大的工作

Since you are new here, we will give you some light work in the first month.
因為你剛進公司，第一個月我們會先給你一些輕鬆的工作。

1. to be light on one's feet 輕快靈活的

The girl <u>is</u> very agile and <u>light on her feet</u>.

這女孩非常敏捷靈活。

2. to make light of sth 對～不在乎、不以為意

It is shocking that someone could <u>make light of</u> child abuse.

有人可以對虐待兒童不以為意，讓人感到詫異。

3. to make light work of sth 迅速輕鬆完成某事

A rice cooker <u>makes light work of</u> cooking for students abroad.

電鍋讓留學生做菜變得輕鬆簡單。

4. to travel light 帶少量的行李旅行

The website provides you with some helpful advice on <u>traveling light</u>.

這網站提供你一些對輕便旅行有幫助的建議。

5. (as) light as a feather 像羽毛一樣輕、輕如鴻毛

His luggage is <u>as light as a feather</u>.

他的行李輕如鴻毛。

6. light and airy 明亮通風的

The room is <u>light and airy</u>. 這房間明亮又通風。

7. on a lighter note / in a lighter vein 說點輕鬆的

<u>On a lighter note</u>, Ed Sheeran will do his Asia tours next month.

說點輕鬆的，紅髮艾德下個月要展開亞洲巡迴演唱會。

Loose

寬鬆的、鬆動的；不受控制的；零散的；不嚴謹的、大略的

▶ MP3-089

loose connection 接觸不良

No wonder your hairdryer isn't working. There's a <u>loose connection</u> in the plug.
插頭的地方接觸不良，難怪你的吹風機不會運作。

loose ball （籃球、美式足球等）球權不屬於任一隊的球（常用於 loose ball foul，指攻守雙方均無持球權時的犯規）

Jeremy Lin dove on the floor for the <u>loose ball</u>, ultimately resulting in a jump ball.
林書豪撲在地上搶球，最後被裁判判定為爭球。

loose tongue 大嘴巴

Thanks to his <u>loose tongue</u>, everyone knows the secret now.
因為他的大嘴巴，現在大家都知道這個祕密了。

loose change 零錢

I would like to empty my pocket of the <u>loose change</u>.
我想把口袋裡的零錢清一清。

loose arrangement 鬆散的安排

We came to some sort of <u>loose arrangement</u> before we headed home.
在回家之前，我們想到了一些鬆散的行程安排。

loose interpretation 不嚴謹的解釋

The lawyer strongly argued that the <u>interpretation</u> of the law was <u>loose</u>.
律師強烈主張那條法律的解釋不夠嚴謹。

loose translation 大略的翻譯

He gave a <u>loose translation</u> of what our French client asked for, so we misunderstood her.
他對法國客戶的要求翻譯有誤，使我們誤解了對方的意思。

實用短語 / 用法 / 句型　　▶ MP3-090

1. **to be at a loose end**　無所事事
   If you find yourself <u>at a loose end</u>, you could clean your bedroom.
   如果你閒著沒事，就把房間清一清。

2. **to break loose**　逃脫、掙脫
   A male inmate <u>broke loose</u> from the sheriff's office yesterday.
   昨天一名男性囚犯從警長室逃走了。

3. **to cut loose** 擺脫束縛、不受控制

I think it's about time your kid <u>cut loose</u> from the family.

我覺得你的小孩是時候要獨立了。

4. **to hang loose** 垂下；（頭髮）披散

The prisoners are so thin that their skin <u>hangs loose</u>.

囚犯瘦到連皮膚都下垂了。

5. **to hang / stay loose** 放輕鬆、冷靜

Let's forget the exam! We'll go to the bar and just <u>hang loose</u> tonight.

忘掉考試吧！我們今晚去酒吧放鬆一下。

6. **to have loose bowels** 拉肚子

He <u>has loose bowels</u> whenever he feels nervous.

他一緊張就會拉肚子。

7. **to let loose** 突然失控地喊出、發出；猛烈開火

She turned around and <u>let loose</u> a torrent of abuse.

她轉過身來破口大罵。

The allies <u>let loose</u> an intensive bombardment over the border.

聯軍對邊境進行猛烈砲擊。

8. to let sb loose (on sth) 放任某人（使用～）

You shouldn't <u>let</u> such a little kid <u>loose on</u> knives.
你不應該放任一個這麼小的孩子玩刀。

The director <u>let</u> his actors <u>loose</u> to interpret their roles in any way they see fit.
導演讓演員用他們認為適合的方式去詮釋角色。

9. to let / set sth loose 鬆開（動物）

He <u>let</u> his dog <u>loose</u> on the beach.
他把狗鬆開，讓牠在海灘上自由奔跑。

10. to tie up loose ends 完成收尾工作、搞定零碎瑣事

The writer <u>ties up all the loose ends</u> at the end of the story.
作者在故事最後把所有零散的情節都串連起來。

11. all hell breaks loose
頓時亂成一團（特別是人群突然爭吵、打鬥起來）

One policeman drew his gun and then suddenly <u>all hell broke loose</u>.
一名員警拔槍，抗議群眾頓時亂成一團。

Low
低的、矮的；（地位、程度）低的、卑微的；消沉的、低落的；含量低的

▶ MP3-091

low bow　深深的鞠躬

The president made a <u>low bow</u> to the veterans of the Vietnam War.
總統向越戰老兵鞠躬致敬。

low achiever　成就、表現不佳的人

Not enough attention is given to the <u>low achievers</u> in the class.
班上成績不好的人不太受重視。

low expectations　低期望、期望不高

College graduates nowadays have <u>low expectations</u> for their future.
如今大學畢業生對未來的期望不高。

low light　低亮度、光線昏暗

Many cafes tend to use <u>low lights</u> and soft music to create a relaxed and romantic atmosphere.
很多咖啡廳喜歡用昏暗的燈光和柔和的音樂來營造輕鬆浪漫的氣氛。

low opinion　評價不高

A growing number of teenagers have <u>low opinions</u> of the tabloid newspapers.
越來越多年輕人對八卦報紙給予負評。

low point （活動、期間的）最低點、最糟的時候

The time when we were separated in two different countries was the low point in our relationship.
分隔兩地的日子是我們關係最糟的時候。

low priority 不重要

A missing wallet or a missing bicycle is a low priority for police.
錢包遺失或是腳踏車失竊對警方來說並不屬於優先處理的案件。

low profile 不引人注目的姿態、低調

I've been in a little trouble recently so I'm trying to keep a low profile.
我最近碰上了一些麻煩，所以試圖保持低調。

low spirits 情緒低落

David somehow seems to be in rather low spirits today.
大衛今天不知道為什麼心情似乎相當低落。

low season 淡季

Some employees would take other work in the low season to guarantee a steady income.
有些員工在淡季時會兼差來確保自己有穩定的收入。

1. to be / get / run low (on sth)

缺乏、不足、耗盡（某物）

We're <u>running low on</u> oil. I suggest that we stop by the gas station.

我們快沒油了，我建議去一下加油站。

2. to be low in sth　某物的含量低

People who are on a diet are recommended to eat food that <u>is low in</u> calories.

在減肥的民眾建議吃低熱量的食物。

3. to be low on the list (of priorities)

非當務之急、不重要

Customer service <u>is low on the list of</u> the company's <u>priorities</u>, but actually good service can be the key to higher sales.

這間公司不重視顧客服務，但事實上好的服務卻是提升銷售量的關鍵。

4. to lie low　保持低調

In this situation, you should <u>lie low</u> instead of being outspoken.

在這種情況下，你應該保持低調，不該直言不諱。

5. 「in the low + 數字 s」　～出頭，舉例來說 in the low 40s，就是數字略高於 40 卻不到 45

Temperatures in most areas in Taiwan will be <u>in the low tens</u> tomorrow.

明天台灣多數地區的氣溫只有 10 度出頭。

Major   主要的、重大的；大部分的；主修的

▶ MP3-093

major accident / incident   重大的意外、事故

The government is investing a huge amount of money in the emergency services to enable them to better respond to <u>major incidents</u>.
政府在緊急服務上投入大量資金，使其能更快速應對重大事故。

major breakthrough / milestone   重大的突破 / 里程碑

The new deal represents a <u>major milestone</u> for our company.
這項新協議對我們公司來説，是個重大的里程碑。

major cause / factor   主要的因素

Most people agree that money is a <u>major cause</u> of stress for today's family.
多數人都同意，錢是現代家庭壓力的主要來源。

major challenge / hurdle / obstacle   主要的挑戰、阻礙

The negative attitude of the opposition party proved to be a <u>major obstacle</u> to passing the act.
在野黨的反對會是通過該法案的一大挑戰。

major concern 主要的考量、關注問題

Preventing road accidents is the government's <u>major concern</u>.
避免道路事故是政府主要關注的問題。

major conflict / confrontation 重大的衝突

This is not a permanent solution, and sooner or later it will provoke a <u>major confrontation</u>.
這不是一個長久之計，它遲早會引發重大衝突。

major contribution 重大的貢獻

These two papers published in 1995 together made a <u>major contribution</u> to the study of positive psychology.
這兩篇 1995 年發表的論文對正向心理學的研究有非常大的貢獻。

major drawback / flaw 主要的缺點

The trip sounds great, but its high cost is a <u>major drawback</u>.
這趟旅程聽起來不錯，但它的費用太高，是主要的缺點。

major impact / influence 重大的影響

We expect the amount of sleep will have a <u>major impact</u> on people's physical and mental health.
我們認為睡眠量會對人類的身心健康造成重大影響。

major importance 極其重要

Railways were of <u>major importance</u> in opening up the American West.
鐵路對美國西部的開發極其重要。

major part / role 主要的部分、重要的角色

Market research plays a <u>major part</u> in gaining insight into customers' needs.
市場研究在了解顧客需求上扮演重要的角色。

major problem / setback 重大的問題／打擊

The loss of its goalkeeper through injury will be a <u>major setback</u> for the team.
守門員因傷退賽將會對球隊造成重大打擊。

major program / project / undertaking
重大的計畫／任務

During the 2000s, the city underwent a <u>major</u> urban renewal <u>project</u>.
在 2000 到 2010 年間，這個城市歷經了重大的都市更新。

major road 主要的道路、幹道

The <u>major road</u> to the city was closed due to the typhoon.
因為颱風的影響，通往城市的主要道路被迫封閉。

major overhaul / redevelopment / refit /
refurbishment / repair 大範圍檢修 / 重建 / 改裝 / 整修 / 修理

Our systems undergo a <u>major overhaul</u> on a regular basis.
我們的系統定期做大規模檢修。

major shake-up （人員）大改組

In a <u>major shake-up</u>, the airlines cut hundreds of jobs.
航空公司在重大人事變動中裁減了數百個職位。

Massive 巨大的；大量的、巨額的；大規模的；（病情）嚴重的

▶ MP3-094

massive blow 巨大的打擊

The player's serious injury would be a <u>massive blow</u> to the team's championship hopes.

這位球員受了嚴重的傷，這對球隊的冠軍夢是一大打擊。

massive change 巨大的改變

Only <u>massive changes</u> in government policies will prevent the economy from going into recession.

唯有大幅修改政府的政策，才能避免經濟衰退。

massive effect / impact 巨大的影響

The president's offensive remarks had a <u>massive impact</u> on the company.

總裁的失言對公司造成嚴重影響。

massive bill 巨額的帳單

A <u>massive</u> tax <u>bill</u> can be devastating to a family budget.

巨額的稅單對家庭預算來説會是一大災難。

massive bleeding 大量出血

The driver had <u>massive bleeding</u> in the terrible car accident.

這場嚴重車禍中，駕駛大量出血。

massive boost / growth / increase 大量增加、成長

There have been <u>massive increases</u> in the prices of many
daily necessities.
許多日用品的價格大幅上漲。

massive debt 巨額的負債

The new government's main aim is to tackle the country's
<u>massive debt</u>.
新政府的主要目標是解決國家的巨額負債。

massive effort 大量的努力

A <u>massive effort</u> will be required to clean up the debris after
the typhoon.
颱風過後,清理這些瓦礫相當費力。

massive influx 大量湧入

Many Germans are worried about the impact of the <u>massive
influx</u> of refugees on their economy.
許多德國人擔心大量的難民潮對其經濟所造成的影響。

massive investment 大量投資

The figures show that this developing country needs
<u>massive investment</u> in its energy, transportation, and urban
infrastructure.
數據顯示這個發展中國家的能源、運輸和都市的基礎建設需要大量
的投資。

massive earthquake / explosion 大地震 / 大爆炸

Countless people were killed in the <u>massive earthquake</u> in Japan that triggered a devastating tsunami.
日本的大地震造成無數居民死亡，還引發毀滅性的海嘯。

massive expansion 大規模擴張

The company is now ready to embark on <u>massive expansion</u> overseas.
公司準備要在海外大規模擴張。

massive hit / success 大成功（= huge hit / success）

The Coldplay concert in Taiwan last week was a <u>massive success</u>.
酷玩樂團上星期在台灣的演唱會非常成功。

massive retaliation 大規模的復仇

They are afraid that military action would likely trigger <u>massive retaliation</u> and casualties.
他們擔心軍事行動可能引發大規模的報復和死傷。

massive scale 大規模

If the drought continues, deaths will occur on a <u>massive scale</u>.
如果乾旱持續，將會有大量民眾死亡。

massive task / undertaking 繁重的工作、浩大的工程

The Brazilian government has turned its attention to the <u>massive task</u> of preparing for the world's biggest sports event.

巴西政府已經將注意力轉移到全球最大的體育盛事的浩大準備工程上。

massive heart attack / stroke 嚴重的心臟病 / 中風

A few days ago his grandfather died of a <u>massive heart attack</u>.

他爺爺幾天前因為心臟病發過世了。

Minor 次要的、不重要的、不嚴重的；小部分的；副修的；未成年的

▶ MP3-095

minor accident / incident 輕微的事故

The firefighters managed to prevent a <u>minor accident</u> from turning into a major blaze.
消防員設法阻止一場小事故演變成重大火災。

minor ailment / illness / injury 輕微的疾病、小病 / 傷勢

Pharmacists are a good source of advice about <u>minor ailments</u>.
藥劑師能針對小病給一些不錯的建議。

minor breach / crime / offense 輕微觸法、輕罪

Teenagers under eighteen will not be sent to prison for <u>minor offenses</u>.
18 歲以下的青少年不會因為輕微案件被關。

minor bug / defect / drawback / fault / flaw
小瑕疵、小缺點

A product having a <u>minor flaw</u> that does not impair its use is usually sold at a discount.
只要小瑕疵不影響使用，商品通常會折價出售。

minor complaint / gripe / quibble 小牢騷、小抱怨

Those are just <u>minor quibbles</u> about the cover of the magazine.
那些只是對雜誌封面的小抱怨。

minor error / mistake / problem / setback
小錯誤 / 問題 / 挫折

The manager is not going to give him the hook just because he made a <u>minor mistake</u>.
經理不會因為他犯了一個小錯就開除他。

minor importance 不大重要

The rest is of <u>minor importance</u>, so let's move on to the next chapter.
剩下的部分不大重要，讓我們進到下一章。

minor inconvenience 小小的不方便

For most Americans, changing the clocks twice a year is a <u>minor inconvenience</u>.
對大部分的美國人來說，每年要調整兩次時間有點不方便。

minor part / role 小部分、不重要的角色

I just occupied a <u>minor role</u> in bringing about the reforms.
我在推動這次的改革上只扮演了一個小角色。

minor road 支道

The map is very detailed, with all paths and <u>minor roads</u> shown.
這份地圖的資訊非常詳細，標出了所有鄉間小路和支道。

minor adjustment / alteration / amendment / modification / revision / tweak 微幅調整、修改

We made <u>minor adjustments</u> to our draft before giving a presentation.
在報告前，我們稍微修改了一下草稿。

minor difference / discrepancy 細微的差異

The officer failed to notice the <u>minor discrepancy</u> between the name on the ticket and that on the passport.
海關人員沒有注意到機票和護照上姓名的細微差異。

minor child 未成年子女

In order to protect the rights of <u>minor children</u>, the system of parents' support for <u>minor children</u> after divorce should be improved.
為了保障未成年子女的權利，父母離異後孩子的扶養制度應有所改善。

Moderate

中等的、適度的、有節制的；溫和的、不偏激的

▶ MP3-096

moderate activity / exercise 適度的運動

Moderate exercise with a balanced diet can help to prevent heart disease.
適度運動搭配均衡飲食有助於預防心臟病。

moderate amount / degree / level / number 適量、

適度（amount 修飾不可數名詞；number 修飾可數名詞）

While a moderate amount of stress can be beneficial, too much stress can stifle kids' creativity.
雖然適量的壓力是有益的，但過多的壓力反而會扼殺小孩的創意。

moderate change / improvement 略微改變 / 改善

There has been a moderate improvement in his health since he began the treatment.
開始接受治療後，他的健康狀況已經略有好轉。

moderate charge / cost / price / rent

中等的費用 / 成本 / 價格 / 租金

It is hard to find a hotel offering comfortable rooms at moderate prices in Taipei.
在台北很難用中等價位找到提供舒適房間的飯店。

moderate climate / rain / rainfall / temperature

溫和的氣候 / 適度的降雨 / 適中的溫度

Areas of yellow on the map indicate moderate rainfall.
地圖上的黃色區域代表中等的降雨量。

moderate consumption / drinking / intake

適度的食用 / 飲用 / 攝取

The study indicates that a moderate intake of caffeine should not harm people.
研究指出，適度攝取咖啡因不會對人體造成傷害。

moderate damage　中等程度的損害

The store had suffered moderate damage when firefighters arrived.
在消防隊員趕到火場時，這家店已經受了一定程度的損害。

moderate dose　適度的劑量

Most patients suffer no ill effects from the moderate dose of the drug.
適度劑量的藥物在大多數病患身上不會造成不良影響。

moderate effect / impact　中等的、不嚴重的影響

Some experts believe that Brexit could have a moderate effect on the U.S. economy.
部分專家認為英國脫歐對美國經濟造成的影響可能不嚴重。

moderate growth / increase / inflation

適度的成長、增加 / 通膨

A <u>moderate increase</u> in body temperature is not a big deal.
體溫適度升高不是什麼大問題。

moderate heat 適中的火候、溫度

Make sure you cook the steak over a <u>moderate heat</u>.
你一定要用中火煎牛排。

moderate income 中等收入

It is impossible for a family with a <u>moderate income</u> to buy a house in Taipei City.
對於一個中等收入的家庭來說，要在台北市買房是不可能的。

moderate intensity 中等強度

Current research suggests that 30 minutes of <u>moderate-intensity</u> activities every day is enough to improve health.
最近的研究指出，每天 30 分鐘中等強度的運動能夠改善健康狀況。

moderate pace / speed 中等速度

We prefer to tour the museum at a <u>moderate pace</u>.
我們希望能悠閒地參觀這間博物館。

moderate size 中等大小

The cabin is of <u>moderate size</u>—just right for a small family.
這間小木屋的大小適中，正好適合一個小家庭。

moderate success 略微成功、小有成就

We have had <u>moderate success</u> in changing people's methods for learning languages.
在改變民眾學習語言的方式上，我們已經略有成就。

moderate approach 溫和的方式

Both countries have called for a <u>moderate approach</u> to settling disputes.
兩個國家都呼籲用溫和的方式解決紛爭。

moderate opinion / view 溫和的、不偏激的意見

This senator holds <u>moderate</u> political <u>opinions</u>.
這位參議員抱持不偏激的政治觀點。

Pathological 不受控制的、病態的、非理性的；疾病的 ▶ MP3-097

pathological behavior 病態的行為

The leader's <u>pathological behavior</u> makes the political circumstances more dangerous.
領導人病態的行為使政治環境更加危險。

pathological gambler / gambling
賭博成癮的人 / 賭博成癮

Some say that smartphone addiction resembles <u>pathological gambling</u>.
有人認為手機成癮就像賭博成癮一樣。

pathological liar 說謊成性的人

He is a <u>pathological liar</u>; nothing of what he brags about is true.
他說謊成性，吹噓的事情沒有一個是真的。

pathological change 病變

The <u>pathological changes</u> of lungs deserve particular attention.
肝的病變值得特別留意。

pathological examination 病理檢查

There is a suspicious lump in your breast and it needs to undergo a <u>pathological examination</u>.

你的乳房有一個可疑腫塊，需要再做病理檢查。

Perennial 長期的、不斷發生的 ▶ MP3-098

perennial debate 長期的爭論

Another <u>perennial debate</u> pertains to whether or not the world needs a universal language.
另一個長久以來的爭論是，這個世界需不需要一個共通語言。

perennial favorite 歷久不衰、一直以來的喜愛

The menu changes monthly, but the lobster bisque is a <u>perennial favorite</u>.
菜單每個月都會更換，但是龍蝦湯一直以來都深受顧客喜愛。

perennial issue / problem / question 長期的問題 / 疑問

We face the <u>perennial problem</u> of not having enough resources.
我們長期以來都面臨資源不足的問題。

perennial struggle 長期的鬥爭

Species are engaged in a <u>perennial struggle</u> with the ever-changing environment.
物種長期對抗不斷改變的環境。

Poisonous

有毒的、有害的；令人極不愉快的、惡意的

▶ MP3-099

poisonous chemicals / gas / substance

有毒化學物 / 氣體 / 物質

Thousands of fish were killed as a result of the discharge of poisonous chemicals from a nearby factory.
鄰近的工廠將有毒化學物質排放到河中，造成數千條魚死亡。

poisonous plant / snake　有毒的植物 / 毒蛇

Experienced climbers know how to distinguish between a poisonous snake and a harmless one.
有經驗的登山客知道如何分辨毒蛇和無害的蛇。

poisonous atmosphere　險惡的、令人不愉快的氛圍

The rumor created a poisonous atmosphere of suspicion and mistrust.
謠言造成了猜忌和不信任的險惡氛圍。

Prolific 多產的、作品豐富的

▶ MP3-100

prolific writer 多產的作家

Steven Pinker is widely known as a prolific writer in the field of psychology.
史迪芬平克以他心理學領域的大量著作聞名。

prolific producer 產量多的製造者、生產源頭

The Golden River was once a prolific producer of salmon.
黃金河流曾經盛產鮭魚。

prolific journalist 多產的新聞記者

Kevin was known as a prolific journalist, having written a plethora of articles, reviews, and books.
凱文以一個多產的新聞記者聞名,撰寫過許多文章、評論和書。

Promising 有希望的、有前途的　▶ MP3-101

promising approach / avenue / direction / line / method / route / strategy / technique / way
有希望的方法、途徑

Genetically modified food is seen as a <u>promising approach</u> to tackling food shortage.
基改食物被視為解決糧食短缺的可能方法。

His research suggested several <u>promising lines</u> of investigation.
他的研究提出了幾個有希望的調查方向。

promising beginning / start　好的開始

After a <u>promising start</u>, the project soon fizzled out.
這項計畫一開始很有希望，但過沒多久就失敗了。

promising candidate / newcomer / player / prospect / talent 有前途的候選人 / 新人 / 選手 / 人選 / 人才

Eventually, the choices were whittled down to a small number of <u>promising candidates</u>.
最後，選項限縮為少數幾個前景看好的人選。

promising career 有前途的職業

My grandfather gave up a promising career in law to fight for his country.
爺爺為了替國家奮戰，放棄前途光明的法律工作。

promising debut 有希望的首次亮相

The ending isn't convincing, but this is a highly promising debut.
雖然結局不夠有說服力，但首演就能如此，未來非常有希望。

promising future / prospects 美好的前景

Her talent and ability to think critically have become her ticket to a bright and promising future.
她的才能和批判性思考的能力，已經成為她通往光明未來的門票。

promising results 有希望的、有成效的結果

The drug has shown promising results in mice with diabetes.
這種藥物在患有糖尿病的老鼠身上反應良好。

promising sign 良好的跡象

It is a promising sign that our government has already come up with some laws and regulations.
我們的政府已經想出一些法律規範，這是一個好跡象。

Prompt 即時的、迅速的

▶ MP3-102

prompt assistance 即時協助

I appreciate your prompt technical assistance in the project.
我很感謝你對這個計畫即時的技術支援。

prompt attention 即時關注、即時處理

Your prompt attention to this matter would be highly appreciated.
您若能即時處理此事,我們將非常感激。

prompt delivery 即期(快速)交貨、限時郵件

Our company guarantees prompt delivery of goods.
我們公司保證快速到貨。

prompt diagnosis / treatment 及早診斷 / 治療

Prompt diagnosis and treatment are important to prevent progression of disease.
及早診斷和治療對防止病情發展非常重要。

prompt payment 立即付清、即期付款

Many customers are taking advantage of the 2.5% discount for prompt payment.
很多顧客會一次付清來享有 2.5% 的折扣。

prompt reply / response 即時回覆

Thank you for your <u>prompt reply</u> to my e-mail yesterday.
感謝您昨天即時回信。

prompt service 即時服務

We offer <u>prompt</u> after-sales <u>service</u> on all our goods.
我們所有的商品都提供即時的售後服務。

Quick 快速的、立即的；聰敏的

quick decision 快速的決定

We need to make a <u>quick decision</u> now; otherwise the investors will lose confidence in our company.
我們必須快點決定，否則投資人將對公司失去信心。

quick drink 小酌一杯

We had a <u>quick drink</u> at the bar and he dropped me off at my house.
我們在酒吧小酌了一下，他就送我回家。

quick fix 權宜之計（為了應付某些情況而暫時採用的辦法，但不是最好或永久的辦法）

We do not believe that there is a <u>quick fix</u> for the coal industry.
我們不認為有任何權宜之計能解決煤炭工業的問題。

quick glance / look 掃視、匆匆看一眼

He took one last <u>quick look</u> at the room and left.
他最後匆匆看了房間一眼就離開。

quick learner / study 學習能力強、學習速度快的人

He is a <u>quick learner</u>, learning his way around new subject areas fast.
他的學習能力很強，能快速學習新的領域。

quick profit 快速獲利

The investors feel the need to make <u>quick profits</u>.
投資人想要快速獲利。

quick temper 脾氣暴躁（形容詞為 quick-tempered）

I have a <u>quick temper</u>, and my way of controlling it is to avoid responding or talking to people.
我的脾氣暴躁，我控制自己情緒的方法就是不要回應對方。

quick wit 機智（形容詞為 quick-witted）

His friends admire his <u>quick wit</u>. He is always able to defuse tension in the meetings.
他朋友都欣賞他的聰明機智。他總是能緩和會議上緊張的氣氛。

1.　to be quick off the mark 反應快速，如果一個人反
應很慢，我們可以説 to be slow off the mark

The police <u>were quick off the mark</u> in reaching the
scene of the accident.
警察迅速抵達事故現場。

2.　to be quick on the draw 反應快速；拔槍迅速

She <u>was quick on the draw</u> and calmly responded
to the reporter's questions.
她反應很快，冷靜回答了記者的問題。

3.　to be quick on the uptake 理解得很快、理解力強，
相反地，如果一個人理解得很慢，則可以説 to be slow
on the uptake

He <u>is not quick on the uptake</u>, so you may have to
explain the situation in concrete terms.
他的理解力不好，所以你可能要用具體的方式説明狀
況。

4.　to cut someone to the quick
戳到某人痛處、傷了某人

Her acerbic remark <u>cut me to the quick</u>.
她脱口而出的尖酸話語深深傷了我。

5.　(as) quick as a flash / wink 快如閃電、非常快速

The customers are complaining. We need to get
food ready <u>as quick as a flash</u>.
顧客一直抱怨，我們必須快點把食物準備好。

Rapid 快速的、迅速的

▶ MP3-105

rapid advance / development / progress / progression 快速進步、迅速發展

This change enables our teachers to develop students' abilities so that they make rapid progress.
這項改變使我們的老師能開發學生的能力，學生因此進步飛快。

rapid change 快速改變

We are living in a time of incredibly rapid change.
我們生活在一個變化快速的時代。

rapid decline / deterioration 快速下降、迅速惡化

There was a rapid decline in the fortunes of the Taiwanese film industry.
台灣電影工業的資產快速減少。

rapid expansion / growth / increase / rise / spread 快速增長

During the nineteenth century there was a rapid expansion of large-scale industries.
大型工業在 19 世紀時快速擴張。

There has been rapid growth in the number of new businesses in the city.
都市的新公司數量迅速增加。

rapid recovery 迅速恢復（= speedy recovery）

The solider made a <u>rapid recovery</u> from his injury.
這位士兵很快就傷癒了。

rapid spread 迅速蔓延

Close contact between people resulted in the <u>rapid spread</u> of SARS.
人與人的近距離接觸，導致嚴重急性呼吸道症候群的疫情迅速蔓延。

實用短語 / 用法 / 句型　　　　　▶ MP3-106

1. **at a rapid pace / rate** 很快的速度
   Deforestation is occurring <u>at a rapid pace</u> as a result of agricultural development.
   因為農業的發展，森林被快速砍伐。

2. **in rapid succession** 緊接地、接連地
   The family moved several times <u>in rapid succession</u>.
   這家人接連搬了好幾次家。

Rash 草率的、魯莽的

▶ MP3-107

rash action 魯莽的行動

Our <u>rash actions</u> resulted in a serious accident that caused casualties.
我們魯莽的行動導致了嚴重的意外，造成人員傷亡。

rash challenge 惡意犯規（足球）

He was incredibly fortunate not to be sent off at the first half for a <u>rash challenge</u>.
他非常幸運沒有因為惡意犯規而在上半場被驅逐出場。

rash decision 魯莽的決定

Before making any <u>rash decisions</u> about your future, you should consider the following points.
對未來做魯莽決定前，你必須想想以下幾點。

rash promise 草率的承諾

He made a <u>rash promise</u> that he would soon regret.
他草率做出很快就會後悔的承諾。

1. **It is rash of sb to do sth** 某人做某事很魯莽

   I think <u>it was</u> a bit <u>rash of</u> them <u>to get</u> married when they'd only known each other for a few days.

   他們才剛認識沒幾天就結婚，我覺得這有點魯莽。

Relentless 持續的

▶ MP3-109

relentless campaign 持續的宣傳運動

The Islamic State's <u>relentless</u> media <u>campaigns</u> have fueled a global migration of militants.
伊斯蘭國持續的媒體宣傳，吸引了全球激進分子紛紛前去。

relentless demand 無盡的需求

Sharks are critically endangered partly because of people's <u>relentless demand</u> for their fins.
鯊魚嚴重瀕臨絕種，部分原因是人類對魚翅的無盡需求。

relentless determination 持續的決心

The athlete showed her <u>relentless determination</u> to succeed.
這位運動員展現出不屈不撓想要成功的決心。

relentless effort 持續的努力

The government has made a <u>relentless effort</u> to provide people with safe and affordable houses.
政府持續努力為民眾提供安全且負擔得起的房子。

relentless heat 持續的高溫

The ultramarathon runners had to endure the <u>relentless heat</u> of the desert.
超級馬拉松選手必須忍受沙漠持續的高溫。

relentless pressure 持續的壓力

The airlines are facing <u>relentless pressure</u> to lay off workers.
航空公司持續面臨裁員的壓力。

relentless pursuit 持續的追求

Success follows <u>relentless pursuit</u> of something you believe in.
成功來自堅持不懈地追求你所相信的事物。

Rigorous 嚴格的、嚴謹的

▶ MP3-110

rigorous training 嚴格的訓練

The runner did six months' <u>rigorous training</u> before the marathon.
跑者在馬拉松比賽前，進行了 6 個月的嚴格訓練。

rigorous analysis / assessment / evaluation / testing 嚴密的分析 / 評估 / 測試

We went through a very <u>rigorous testing</u> and <u>assessment</u> process.
我們歷經了非常嚴密的測試和評估過程。

rigorous approach / method / methodology / process 嚴謹的方法

We should apply <u>rigorous</u> scientific <u>methodologies</u> to questions that are relevant to a wide range of diseases.
我們應該把嚴謹的科學方法應用到廣泛疾病的相關問題上。

rigorous checks / examination / inspection / investigation 嚴格的檢查 / 調查

We ran <u>rigorous checks</u> on the quality of our ingredients.
我們對原料的品質進行了嚴格檢查。

rigorous control 嚴格的控制

There are <u>rigorous controls</u> governing the sale of shares in the company.
公司對股票的出售有嚴格管控。

rigorous criteria / standards 嚴格的標準

The <u>criteria</u> are <u>rigorous</u> and all criteria must be fulfilled to achieve the award.
這些標準很嚴格，而且必須所有的條件都符合才能獲獎。

rigorous monitoring / scrutiny 嚴格的監控 / 審查

The firm is conducting a <u>rigorous monitoring</u> in order to reduce the staff costs.
為了降低人事成本，公司正在進行嚴格的監控。

rigorous process 嚴格的過程

Due to the extremely <u>rigorous process</u>, errors in the data are rare.
由於極其嚴格的過程，數據中的錯誤非常少。

rigorous proof 嚴格的證據

The judge laid particular emphasis on the need for clear and <u>rigorous proof</u>.
法官特別強調需要明確嚴格的證據。

rigorous study 縝密的研究

There is a need to undertake <u>rigorous studies</u> to assess, identify and quantify the possible impacts of climate change on wild animals.

有必要進行縝密的研究來評估、確認、量化氣候變遷對野生動物可能造成的影響。

Robust 健壯的、健全的;強勁的、堅定的、果決的;

濃郁的、濃烈的 ▶ MP3-111

robust economy / system 強健的經濟 / 健全的系統

The Trump administration vowed to maintain a robust economy.
川普政府誓言要維持強健的經濟。

robust health 健壯的身體

To be an astronaut, you must be in robust health.
要成為太空人,你必須要有強健的身體。

robust approach 果決的、強硬的手段

The police are taking a more robust approach toward the
protesters, who have become more aggressive.
抗議人士的行為已經越來越激烈,警方開始對他們採取更強硬的手
段。

robust defense 強力的辯護

The minister of foreign affairs made a robust defense of the
agreement.
外交部長為此協議強力辯護。

robust performance 強勁的表現

It is expected that the US housing market will maintain its
<u>robust performance</u> next year.
美國房地產市場預期明年將延續強勁的表現。

robust flavor 濃烈的味道

The specialty cheese plays well to consumer desires for
foods with more <u>robust</u> and unique <u>flavors</u>.
這個特色起司大大滿足那些鍾愛濃烈且獨特風味食物的消費者。

Rough

粗糙的、崎嶇的；粗略的；艱難的、難受的；粗製的、未加工的；粗暴的、粗俗的；（天氣、海象）惡劣的

▶ MP3-112

rough edges 待改進之處、不完美的地方（也可以說 to be rough around the edges）

He's a great player, but his performance still has a few <u>rough edges</u>.
他是很棒的選手，但表現仍有待改進之處。

rough approximation 粗略、大概的近似值

Could you give us a <u>rough approximation</u> of the cost?
你能告訴我們大約的成本嗎？

rough calculation / estimate 粗略的計算 / 估計

We will produce a <u>rough estimate</u> of what we think the work will cost.
我們會粗略估計我們認為這次工作所需的成本。

rough draft / outline 粗略的草稿、大綱

This document is a <u>rough outline</u> of the discussion we have had.
這份文件是我們討論過程的粗略大綱。

rough guess 粗略猜測

At a <u>rough guess</u>, this pair of shoes will cost some five thousand dollars.
粗略猜測，這雙鞋要 5,000 元左右。

rough guide 粗略的指導

It should be considered a <u>rough guide</u> because it may differ in individuals.
這應該被當作粗略的指導，因為它可能因人而異。

rough idea 粗略的、大致的想法

She has got only a <u>rough idea</u> as to what this trip will be.
她對這趟旅行只有粗略的想法。

rough sketch 草圖

The architect did a <u>rough sketch</u> of what the new office would look like.
設計師大概畫了一下新辦公室的草圖。

rough day / time
艱困的日子、時期（也可以說 tough day / time）

Since his wife died, he has been having a <u>rough time</u>.
自從太太去世，他的日子就很不好過。

rough deal 不公平的、不愉快的遭遇

She's had a <u>rough deal</u> with her boyfriend leaving her like that.
她男朋友就這樣離開她，對她並不公平。

rough going 艱難的過程、困境（也可以説 tough going）

When he tried to implement a few changes at his job, he found it <u>rough going</u>.
當他試圖對工作做些改變，卻發現那很困難。

rough night 失眠、睡不好的一夜

I had a <u>rough night</u>, worried about my presentation today.
我昨晚因為擔心今天的口頭報告而失眠。

rough passage / ride 艱難的過程

If you think going to graduate school while working a full-time job is easy, you will be in for a <u>rough ride</u>!
如果你認為邊讀研究所、邊做全職工作是件容易的事，那麼你會經歷一段艱困的日子。

rough sea / weather
惡劣的航行狀況 / 天氣（也可以説 inclement weather）

The <u>sea</u> is too <u>rough</u> for sailing in small boats.
航行狀況太惡劣，不適合小船航行。

1. to be rough on sb 對某人嚴厲、粗暴

Don't you think you <u>were</u> a little too <u>rough on</u> the kid?

你不覺得你對小孩太嚴厲了嗎？

2. to give sb a rough ride 使某人吃苦頭

Journalists <u>gave</u> the prime minister <u>a rough ride</u> at the press conference.

記者讓首相在記者會上吃盡苦頭。

3. to go through a rough patch 經歷艱困的時期

Our marriage <u>went through a rough patch</u> after I lost my job.

我失業之後，我們的婚姻經歷了一段艱困的時期。

4. to take the rough with the smooth

好壞都能接受、順境逆境都能承受

That's relationships—you have to <u>take the rough with the smooth</u>.

感情就是這樣，有好有壞，你必須要都接受。

5. rough and ready 粗略不完美但尚可接受的

I've done a <u>rough and ready</u> translation of the instructions. I hope it's clear enough.

我粗略翻譯了一下使用手冊，希望它夠清楚。

Sensitive 敏感的；易受影響的；機密的；靈敏的

▶ MP3-114

sensitive case / issue / matter / subject / topic
敏感的議題

Most Internet users are worried about their online privacy, especially when it comes to the sensitive subject of their contact information.
多數網路使用者都擔心自己的線上隱私，特別是涉及到聯絡資訊的敏感議題。

sensitive equipment 敏感的儀器、設備

The patient's responses are recorded on a sensitive piece of equipment that gives extremely accurate readings.
病人的反應由一台敏感儀器記錄下來，這個儀器能顯示非常精確的讀數。

sensitive nature 敏感性

Public access to the conference was barred due to the sensitive nature of the topic.
因為話題敏感，一般民眾禁止參加這個會議。

sensitive market 價格、行情易波動的市場

This news directly affects consumer spending and <u>sensitive</u> <u>markets</u> such as housing prices.
這個消息直接影響到消費者的支出，以及像是房地產這樣敏感的市場。

sensitive data / document / information / material
機密資料

<u>Sensitive information</u> such as credit card details and customer records is not held on our website.
機密資料像是信用卡詳情和客戶紀錄等都不會保存在我們的網站上。

sensitive approach / method 靈敏、敏銳的方法

The company asked for a more <u>sensitive approach</u> in handling such cases, but nothing seems to have come out of it.
公司要求在處理這類案例時要用更靈敏的方法，但似乎沒什麼結果。

Serious 重要的；嚴重的；嚴肅的、認真的；大量的、過多的

▶ MP3-115

serious attention / consideration / thought
特別關注、認真考慮

We'll give your suggestion serious consideration.
我們會認真考慮你的建議。

serious business / matter 重要的事情、大事

This is a serious matter that needs to be addressed by all members of the club.
這件事非常重要，必須由全體會員一同處理。

serious breach / crime / offense / violation
嚴重的違法行為

Drunk driving is now a serious offense that could result in a jail sentence.
酒駕現在是嚴重的違法行為，駕駛人可能會被判入獄。

serious challenge / crisis / issue / situation
嚴重的挑戰 / 危機 / 議題 / 狀況

The healthcare system is on the verge of a serious crisis.
醫療體系正瀕臨嚴重危機。

serious consequence 嚴重的後果

It had never crossed his mind that there might be a <u>serious consequence</u>.
他從沒想過會有這麼嚴重的後果。

serious damage 嚴重的損害

The explosion sparked a fire that caused <u>serious damage</u> to their apartment.
這場爆炸引發了大火，對他們的公寓造成嚴重損害。

serious illness / injury 嚴重的疾病／傷

The taxi driver was taken to the hospital with <u>serious injuries</u>.
計程車司機受到重傷，被送往醫院。

serious trouble 嚴重的問題、大麻煩

The new tax regulations have landed some of the smaller companies in <u>serious trouble</u>.
新稅制使一些較小的公司陷入大麻煩。

serious money 為數可觀的金錢

The man started earning <u>serious money</u> by investing in real estate in his fifties.
這男人在 50 多歲時開始投資房地產，賺了一大筆錢。

1. deadly serious 非常嚴肅的

You had better stop making fun of him. He sounds <u>deadly serious</u>.

你最好別再取笑他了，他的語氣聽起來非常嚴肅。

Shaky 搖晃的、顫抖的；不穩定的、不可靠的

▶ MP3-117

shaky voice 顫抖的聲音

It is common that many people give a public speech in a shaky voice.
公開演講時聲音顫抖是常有的事。

shaky economy 不穩定的經濟

The administration is taking these steps to try to improve the country's shaky economy.
政府採取這些措施，試圖改善國家經濟不穩定的局面。

shaky evidence 不可靠、站不住腳的證據

These unreliable claims are based on incomplete, shaky evidence.
這些不可靠的說法是基於不完整、站不住腳的證據上。

shaky foundation / ground 不穩的基礎

I think he's on very shaky ground with that argument.
我認為他那個論點相當站不住腳。

1.　to be shaky on one's feet 站不穩

He's recovering well from his operation, but he's still a little <u>shaky on his feet</u>.

手術後他恢復良好，但走路時仍然有些不穩。

2.　to get off to a shaky start

不好的開始（也可以說 to get off to a bad start，相反的，有好的開始則可以說 to get off to a good start）

The team has performed better lately after <u>getting off to a shaky start</u>.

球隊賽季剛開始的表現不佳，但近期的狀況越來越好。

Sharp
尖的；劇烈的；明顯的；敏銳的、精明的；
尖酸刻薄的

▶ MP3-119

sharp bend / corner / curve / turn
急轉彎（急左 / 右轉彎可以說 sharp left / right）

The car turned over as the driver negotiated a <u>sharp turn</u>.
駕駛在急轉彎時，汽車不慎翻覆。

sharp flavor / taste 強烈的味道

I recommend that you add mustard to give the dressing a
<u>sharper taste</u>.
我建議你可以加上芥末，讓醬汁更有味道。

sharp pain 劇痛

The patient sometimes feels a <u>sharp pain</u> in the chest.
患者有時覺得胸口會劇烈疼痛。

sharp decline / downturn / drop / fall / slowdown
驟降、驟減、大跌

The news triggered the recent <u>sharp fall</u> in share prices.
這個消息導致最近的股價大跌。

sharp difference / distinction 明顯的差別

We can see a sharp distinction between these two players.
我們可以看到這兩位選手的明顯差別。

sharp features 明顯的、深邃的輪廓

The model has sharp features: high cheekbones, prominent nose and a pointy chin.
這位模特兒的輪廓相當深邃，擁有高顴骨、高挺的鼻子還有尖下巴。

sharp increase / rise 驟升、暴增、大漲

The result of the policy was price increases and a sharp rise in unemployment.
這一政策的結果是物價上漲、失業率暴增。

sharp mind 精明的頭腦

She is a professional journalist with an extremely sharp mind.
她是個非常精明的專業記者。

sharp sense of sth 敏銳的～感

A good hound should have a sharp sense of smell.
好的獵犬應該具備敏銳的嗅覺。

sharp criticism / rebuke 嚴厲的批評 / 指責

He delivered a <u>sharp rebuke</u> to those who argued against his opinions.
他嚴厲斥責那些反對他意見的人。

sharp tongue 說話刻薄、毫不留情

He has quite a <u>sharp tongue</u>. Don't be totally unnerved by what he says or the way he says it.
他說話很刻薄，不要太在意他的話或說話的方式。

實用短語 / 用法 / 句型　▶ MP3-120

1. **to be at the sharp end (of sth)**
   （活動、工作）面臨挑戰、困難
   A job like his would be too demanding for me, but he enjoys <u>being at the sharp end</u>.
   像他那樣的工作對我來說太重了，但他就是喜歡挑戰。

2. **to be sharp with sb** 對某人尖酸刻薄
   He <u>was</u> a little <u>sharp with</u> her when she asked him for help.
   當她向他求助時，他講話有點酸。

3. **to keep a sharp eye on sb** 密切注意、留意某人
   Security guards <u>kept a sharp eye on</u> the man as he walked through the store.
   當他走過商店時，保全密切注意他。

4. **(as) sharp as a tack** 非常聰明敏銳的

She may be old in years, but she's still <u>as sharp as a tack</u> and knows what she's talking about.

她可能老了，但她還是非常聰明，知道自己在講什麼。

5. **in sharp contrast to** 與～形成鮮明對比

The kid's cheerful mood stands <u>in sharp contrast to</u> the dreary surroundings.

小孩子愉快的心情和沉悶的環境形成強烈對比。

6. **razor sharp** 非常尖銳的；非常犀利的

Those lawyers are <u>razor sharp</u>, and you've got to be careful about every single word you say.

那些律師非常犀利，你得小心自己講的一字一句。

Significant

重要的、值得注意的；大量的、顯著的

▶ MP3-121

significant achievement / milestone / success
重要的成就

His most significant political achievement was the abolition of the death penalty.
他最重要的政治成就是廢除死刑。

significant action / move 重大的行動

If these steps can't reduce the problems, we will take more significant action.
如果這些手段不能減緩問題，我們將採取更重大的行動。

significant advance / progress / stride
重大的進步、進展

Research in the field has led to significant health advances in the last decade.
這個領域的研究在過去 10 年內帶來了重大的醫療進步。

significant challenge / difficulty / disadvantage / disruption / obstacle 重大的挑戰、難題、阻礙

The country's economy now faces a significant challenge.
這個國家的經濟現在面臨重大挑戰。

significant consequence / implications

重大的結果 / 影響

Brexit has significant implications for the EU economy and for the global economy.
英國脫歐對歐盟及全球經濟都有重大影響。

significant contribution 重大的貢獻

He made a significant contribution to peace in the region.
他為這個地方的和平做了重大貢獻。

significant decision 重大的決定

That is a very significant decision on the question of peace and security.
那是一個和平與安全議題上重大的決定。

significant development 重大的發展

The most significant recent development is the introduction of the Electronic Toll Collection System.
近期最重大的發展是引進電子收費系統。

significant factor 重要的因素

Time appears to be the most significant factor in this whole experiment.
時間似乎是整個實驗中最重要的因素。

significant part / role 重要的角色

Cultural factors play a <u>significant role</u> in the continued reliance of rural communities on traditional medicine.
鄉村之所以會持續依賴傳統療法，文化因素扮演了重要的角色。

significant amount / number / sum

大量（amount / sum 修飾不可數名詞；number 修飾可數名詞）

We have all invested <u>significant amounts</u> of time and energy in doing this project.
我們已經在這項計畫上投入了大量的時間和精力。

significant boost / change / improvement

顯著的、重大的提升 / 改變 / 改善

Please inform us if there are any <u>significant changes</u> in your plans.
如果你的計畫有任何重大改變，麻煩通知我們。

significant decline / decrease / drop / fall / reduction 顯著的減少、下降

The study found a statistically <u>significant decrease</u> in symptoms in patients who had taken the drug.
該研究發現，在統計數據上，服用了這個藥物的病患，症狀有明顯減緩。

significant degree / extent / level 顯著的程度

Our assessment is that our proposal will not increase the cost of goods to any <u>significant extent</u>.
根據我們的評估，提案不會使成本大幅增加。

significant delay 嚴重的延遲

After a <u>significant delay</u>, the government has agreed to accept the recommendations.
歷經嚴重延遲後，政府答應接受這些建議。

significant difference / discrepancy / gap
明顯的不同 / 差距

There is a <u>significant difference</u> between the birthrate now and that ten years ago.
現在的出生率和 10 年前相比大不相同。

significant effect / impact / influence
顯著的效果、影響

The figure shows that volunteer tutoring programs have a <u>significant impact</u> on student achievement.
這份數據顯示，自願的輔導課程對學生的課業成就有顯著影響。

significant expansion / growth / increase / rise
顯著增加、成長

A notable success of the agriculture in India has been the significant expansion in rice production.
印度農業的成功在於其稻米產量大增。

significant proportion 很大的比例

In Australia, foreign students constitute a significant proportion of the higher education cohort.
在澳洲的高等教育學生中，外國學生佔了很大的比例。

significant risk / threat 重大的風險 / 威脅

The report concludes that aviation poses a significant threat to the world's climate.
這份報告的結論是，航空業對全球氣候構成了重大威脅。

significant trend 明顯的趨勢

There has been a significant trend towards online shopping.
線上購物已經是一股潮流。

Slight 小的、細微的

slight adjustment / change / improvement / modification / variation

細微的調整、改變

The doctor says there has been a <u>slight improvement</u> in his condition.
醫生説他的病情已經略微好轉。

slight amount / degree 少量、細微的程度

The value of the research was not affected in the <u>slightest degree</u>.
這份研究的價值一點都不受影響。

slight chance 很小的機會

It seems that the <u>chance</u> of success is very <u>slight</u>.
成功的機會似乎很小。

slight decline / decrease / dip / drop / fall / reduction

略微減少、下降

This report shows a <u>slight decrease</u> in our sales compared with those last month.
這份報告顯示我們的銷售量和上個月相比略有減少。

slight deviation / difference / variation　細微的不同

The policy at the time didn't make the <u>slightest difference</u> in the situation.
當時的政策並沒有對情況造成任何改變。

slight difficulty / problem　小困難、小問題

The first noticeable symptom is a <u>slight difficulty</u> in breathing.
第一個明顯的症狀是呼吸會有些困難。

slight error / mistake　小錯誤

You will be better off looking at the big picture. Do not dwell on <u>slight errors</u>.
你最好把眼光放遠一些，不要執著於小錯誤。

slight hesitation　一絲猶豫

After a <u>slight hesitation</u>, the man began to speak.
這男人猶豫了一下才開口說話。

slight hint / sign　一絲跡象

The cool breeze carries a <u>slight hint</u> of fall in the air.
涼風透露空氣中的一絲秋意。

slight increase / rise 略微增加、上升

Tuitions for future academic years may be subject to a <u>slight increase</u>.
未來學年的學費可能會略微調漲。

實用短語 / 用法 / 句型　　▶ MP3-123

1. **to not have the slightest chance / doubt / idea**
   一點機會 / 懷疑 / 想法都沒有（反諷用法）
   I do <u>not have the slightest idea</u> what they are talking about.
   我一點都不知道他們在講什麼。

2. **not in the slightest**　一點也不
   That gossip does <u>not</u> interest me <u>in the slightest</u>.
   我對那八卦一點都不感興趣。

Slim 苗條的；少許的

▶ MP3-124

slim figure 苗條的身材

The secret of maintaining a <u>slim figure</u> is regular exercise and balanced meals.
維持苗條身材的祕密在於規律運動和均衡飲食。

slim fit 修身款（服飾）

A <u>slim fit</u> makes you look better than a regular one does.
和正常版型相比，修身款讓你看起來更好看。

slim chance 不太可能、機會渺茫

There is only a <u>slim chance</u> that anyone could survive that crash.
要在那場意外中倖存的機會渺茫。

slim margin 微幅、小幅度（也可以說 narrow margin）

This poll shows that Hillary Clinton leads Donald Trump only by a <u>slim margin</u>.
這份民調顯示希拉蕊・柯林頓僅微幅領先唐納・川普。

Smooth
光滑的；平穩的；流暢的、順利的；圓滑的；
（酒、咖啡）順口的 ▶ MP3-125

smooth flight / ride / sailing 平穩的飛行 / 路途 / 航行
（smooth ride / sailing 也能比喻順利的過程）

We had a very smooth flight with no turbulence at all.
我們這趟飛行很平穩，沒有遇到任何亂流。

In fact, the operation of the company was not all smooth sailing.
事實上，這間公司的營運並非一帆風順。

smooth landing 平穩的降落

Despite the inclement weather, the pilot made a smooth landing.
儘管天氣惡劣，機長還是穩穩地把飛機降落在地面。

smooth journey / passage 平順的旅程

Organizing for a smooth journey takes a lot of time and planning.
籌備一趟順利的旅行需要花費大量時間，還要做很多行前規劃。

smooth operation / running 順利的運作

I am responsible for the smooth running of the sales department.
我負責銷售部門的順利運作。

smooth operator / talker 精明圓滑、油嘴滑舌的人

He's such a <u>smooth talker</u>; he can persuade anyone to do anything.
他這人油腔滑調的，能説服任何人去做任何事。

smooth coffee / wine 順口的咖啡 / 酒

This <u>coffee</u> is incredibly <u>smooth</u> and rich.
這咖啡喝起來很順口、味道很濃郁。

實用短語 / 用法 / 句型　　　▶ MP3-126

1. **to wear sth smooth** 磨光、磨平～
   As time goes by, the stone steps have been <u>worn smooth</u>.
   隨著時間過去，石階已經被磨平了。

2. **(as) smooth as silk** 像絲一般光滑的
   The baby's skin is <u>as smooth as silk</u>.
   這嬰兒的皮膚非常光滑。

Soft 軟的、柔滑的；溫和的、軟弱的；柔和的、輕聲的；（市場、貨幣）疲弱的、不穩定的；輕鬆的

▶ MP3-127

soft beverage / drink 軟性、無酒精飲料

Our party will provide soft beverages for those who don't drink.
我們的派對將提供無酒精飲料給不喝酒的人。

soft heart 心軟、富有同情的心

His rather tough exterior hides a very soft and sensitive heart.
他堅強的外表藏著一顆善良敏感的心。

soft loan 低息貸款

Many banks are willing to give college students a soft loan.
許多銀行願意給大學生低息貸款。

soft money

政治獻金（給予某政黨的捐款，而不是直接贊助特定候選人，直接歸入某候選人競選經費的錢則稱為 hard money）

Corporations and celebrities give political parties amounts of soft money to gain benefits.
企業和名人透過捐助政黨政治獻金來獲得好處。

soft music 輕音樂

While I'm working, I like to listen to some <u>soft music</u>.
工作時我喜歡聽些輕音樂。

soft sound / voice 輕聲、柔和的聲音

The actress gave a speech in a <u>soft voice</u>.
女演員用柔和輕細的聲音發表演講。

soft market 蕭條的、疲軟的市場（當商品供給大過於需求）

This product may be good, but it costs a lot of money, which makes it difficult to sell in the <u>soft market</u>.
這項產品或許不錯，但價格太高，在疲軟的市場上很難銷售。

soft option 最輕鬆省事的選項

Taking the <u>soft option</u> won't help your career develop in the long run.
長遠來看，選擇最輕鬆的工作對你的職涯發展不會有幫助。

soft target 輕鬆的、容易攻擊的目標

Major tourist attractions are a <u>soft target</u> for pickpockets.
主要的旅遊景點是扒手容易下手的地方。

soft touch 容易被説服的人，特別是指容易被説服借錢給別人
（也可以説 easy touch）

Amy is a <u>soft touch</u> especially when she needs some help.
艾咪在需要幫忙時特別好説話。

實用短語 / 用法 / 句型　　▶ MP3-128

1. **to be soft on sb** 對某人溫柔、不嚴厲；對某人著迷
   The president said the measure <u>was soft</u> and weak <u>on</u> criminals.
   總統説這手段太溫和，對罪犯不痛不癢。

   The girl has <u>been soft on</u> him for years.
   這女孩已經喜歡他好幾年了。

2. **to have a soft spot for sb** 喜歡某人、對某人有好感
   He <u>has a soft spot for</u> the girl, but doesn't know what to do.
   他對那女孩有好感，但不知道該怎麼做。

3. **to take a soft line on sth / with sb**
   對某事 / 某人寬容、不嚴厲
   Courts have been <u>taking a soft line with</u> young offenders.
   法院對年輕的犯人較寬容。

4. **(as) soft as butter** 非常柔軟的
   The snow at the resort is <u>as soft as butter</u>.
   這個度假勝地的雪非常柔軟。

5. soft in the head 愚蠢的；頭腦發昏的、瘋狂的

I think he is going <u>soft in the head</u>.

我想他頭腦發昏了。

Solid
堅硬的、結實的、實心的；確定的、可信賴的；
不間斷的、持續的；一致的　▶ MP3-129

solid food　固態食物

Pudding was the first <u>solid food</u> he's eaten since his surgery.
布丁是他手術後吃的第一種固態食物。

solid foundation　紮實的基礎、底子

From the program I laid a <u>solid foundation</u> for my interpreting and translating skills.
這門課程奠定了我紮實的口筆譯基礎。

solid performance　精彩的表現

We all thought that he put on a <u>solid performance</u> last night.
我們都認為他昨晚表現得非常精彩。

solid start　好的開始

The team is off to a <u>solid start</u> this year.
這隊今年有一個好的開局。

solid advice　可靠的建言

You can always turn to Peter for <u>solid advice</u>.
你總是可以從彼得那得到可靠的建言。

solid evidence 可信的證據（= strong evidence）

The police provided <u>solid evidence</u> that Jessica committed the crime.
警方提供了證明潔西卡犯罪的可信證據。

solid reputation 可信的聲譽

Our products enjoy a <u>solid reputation</u> and we have clients in over forty countries.
我們的產品享有可信的聲譽，顧客遍布超過 40 個國家。

solid support 一致、強力的支持

The presidential candidate had the <u>solid support</u> of his party.
這位總統候選人從他的政黨那得到一致的支持。

1. to be on solid ground

基於充分的理由、站得住腳，如果形容一個人「on solid ground」，那麼他對於自己所説的話是很有把握的

Jennifer <u>was on solid ground</u> when she accused her boyfriend of cheating on her.

珍妮佛在控訴她男友偷吃這件事情上站得住腳。

2. (as) solid as a rock 穩固如石的；可靠的

Financially, the company is <u>as solid as a rock</u>.

這間公司在財務方面是可靠的。

3. 「solid + 一段時間」 指連續不間斷的一段時間

She was so exhausted that she slept for a <u>solid 8 hours</u>.

她累到連續睡了 8 個小時。

He has been playing video games for <u>10 solid hours</u>.

他已經連續打電玩打了 10 個小時。

Sound
健康的、完好的；合理的、可靠的；穩固的；熟睡的

▶ MP3-131

sound education 良好的教育

Not every child in the world can have a nutritious diet and get a sound education.
並不是世界上所有的小孩都能獲得營養的飲食和良好的教育。

sound mind 健全的心智

It is not clear whether she was of sound mind at the time of the accident.
目前仍不清楚車禍發生當時，她的精神狀況是否正常。

sound policy 健全的政策

The problems of the industry will only be solved by sound economic policies.
只有健全的經濟政策才能解決這個產業的問題。

sound advice 合理的、可靠的建議

It's good to be able to offer clients sound advice.
能為客戶提供可靠的建議是件好事。

sound analysis / assessment / judgement / reasoning 準確的分析 / 評估 / 判斷 / 推論

He has a reputation for sound professional judgement.
他以擁有準確的專業判斷能力聞名。

sound argument / evidence 合理的論證 / 證據

The suspect insisted that he was innocent, but we haven't seen any sound evidence of that.
嫌犯堅稱他是無辜的，但我們還沒看到任何合理的證據。

sound reason 合理的原因

Give me one sound reason and I'll help you.
給我一個合理的原因，我就幫你。

sound base / basis / footing / foundation 穩固的基礎

Sometimes friendship is a sound basis for a good marriage.
有時友誼是良好婚姻的基礎。

sound economy 穩定的經濟

The government devalued the currency to try to maintain a sound economy.
政府使貨幣貶值，試圖維持穩健的經濟。

sound investment 穩健的投資

Government bonds are a <u>sound investment</u>.
政府公債是一種穩健的投資。

sound knowledge / understanding 充分了解

The human resource assistant requires a <u>sound knowledge</u> of the current recruitment system.
人力資源助理必須充分了解目前的招聘制度。

sound sleep 熟睡

The deafening sound woke me out of a <u>sound sleep</u>.
震耳欲聾的聲響把我從熟睡中吵醒。

實用短語 / 用法 / 句型　　▶ MP3-132

1. **(as) sound as a bell** 非常健康；狀況極好
   I thought the screen would break when the cellphone fell, but it is <u>sound as a bell</u>.
   手機掉下去時，我以為螢幕會破掉，但它卻完好如初。

2. **safe and sound** 安然無恙的
   The missing child came back <u>safe and sound</u>.
   失蹤的孩子平安無事地回來了。

Stable 穩定的、平穩的；可靠的、穩重的

▶ MP3-133

stable condition / state 穩定的狀態

While the survivors are in <u>stable condition</u>, they still remain in the hospital.
雖然倖存者的情況已穩定，但仍在醫院。

stable currency / income / inflation / price

穩定的貨幣 / 收入 / 通貨膨脹 / 價格

<u>Inflation</u> is falling and the local <u>currency</u> is becoming more <u>stable</u>.
通貨膨脹正在下降，國內貨幣也漸趨穩定。

stable democracy / government / society

穩定的民主國家 / 政府 / 社會

In order to join the organization, we have to demonstrate that we are a <u>stable democracy</u>.
為了加入這個組織，我們必須證明我們是穩定的民主國家。

stable economy / growth / market

穩定的經濟 / 成長 / 市場

A business needs a strong, <u>stable economy</u> as the basis for innovation and investment.
一間公司需要強健穩定的經濟作為創新和投資的基礎。

stable environment / situation 穩定的環境

We are attempting to establish a <u>stable</u> political <u>environment</u> in which democracy can flourish.
我們試圖建立一個穩定的政治環境，使民主能夠蓬勃發展。

stable foundation / structure 穩定的基礎 / 結構

The program provides a <u>stable foundation</u> for the development of business skills.
這個課程為商業技能打下穩定的基礎。

stable relationship 穩定的關係

I'm happy to have seen them in a <u>stable relationship</u> for years.
我很高興看到他們多年來關係一直很穩定。

Stark 嚴酷的;明顯的、極度的

▶ MP3-134

stark choice 嚴酷的抉擇

The stark choice I face is between moving out or staying here and paying more.
我面臨的嚴酷抉擇是要搬出去或者留下來付更高的房租。

stark reality 嚴酷的現實

The stark reality is that they are operating at a huge loss.
殘酷的事實是他們的營運嚴重虧損。

stark reminder 殘酷的提醒

This tragedy serves as a stark reminder of the dangers of drunk driving.
這場悲劇作為殘酷的提醒,提醒我們酒駕的危險。

stark warning 嚴厲的警告

The man's death is a stark warning to other people about the danger of drugs.
這名男子的死亡對其他人是個嚴厲的警告,讓他們了解毒品的危險性。

stark difference 明顯的差異

There is a <u>stark difference</u> between the way girls and boys talk.
男女生的講話方式明顯不同。

實用短語 / 用法 / 句型　　▶ MP3-135

1. **in stark contrast to** 與～形成明顯對比
   In the suburbs the spacious houses stand <u>in stark contrast to</u> the slums of the city's poor.
   郊區寬敞的房子和城裡的貧民窟形成了明顯對比。

Steep 陡峭的；急劇的；（價格）過高的

▶ MP3-136

steep cuts 大幅削減

The government budget proposal will spell <u>steep cuts</u> for public health.
這個政府預算案意味著將大幅削減公共衛生支出。

steep decline / decrease / dive / drop / drop-off / fall 驟降、驟減、銳減、大跌

Figures show a <u>steep decline</u> in the number of people seeking asylum last year.
數據顯示去年尋求庇護的人數銳減。

steep growth / hike / increase / rise 驟升、暴增、大漲、飛漲

Over the past decade, we have seen a <u>steep rise</u> in the number of young students studying abroad.
過去 10 年來，我們看到出國讀書的年輕學生數大增。

steep charges / fee / price 過高的費用 / 價格

Consumers have to pay relatively <u>steep prices</u> for commodities now.
消費者現在必須支付相對高昂的價格來購買日常用品。

Stiff
硬的、挺的；僵硬的、不自然的；強烈的、激烈的；嚴厲的、艱難的；（價格、代價）高昂的

▶ MP3-137

stiff collar 硬領

A shirt with a stiff collar is more suitable for you.
硬領的襯衫比較適合你。

stiff manner 強硬的態度

We have never liked the woman's stiff manner.
我們從來都不喜歡那女人強硬的態度。

stiff upper lip 沉著堅定、不露情感

As a senior manager, he has to keep a stiff upper lip and remain optimistic.
身為資深經理，他必須沉著冷靜並且保持樂觀。

stiff competition 激烈的競爭

These companies are worried about losing business in the face of stiff competition.
這幾間公司都擔心在激烈的競爭中丟了生意。

stiff drink / whisky 烈酒 / 烈威士忌

Many people are used to having a stiff drink to help them sleep.
很多人習慣喝烈酒幫助睡眠。

stiff opposition / resistance 強烈的反對

The proposed tax increases have encountered <u>stiff opposition</u>.
增加稅收的提案遭到強烈反對。

stiff penalty / punishment / sentence
嚴厲的懲罰 / 判決

The tennis player was given a <u>stiff punishment</u> for using drugs.
這名網球選手因為服用禁藥而受到嚴厲懲罰。

stiff test 嚴峻的測驗

The prime minister is facing a <u>stiff test</u> of his authority.
首相的權威正面臨嚴峻考驗。

stiff fine 高昂的罰款

Drivers who do not obey the rules will face <u>stiff fines</u> of up to NT$9,000.
違反規則的駕駛人將面臨最高新台幣 9,000 元的鉅額罰款。

stiff price 高昂的價格、代價

A new study suggests that states that target the rich for tax hikes may pay a <u>stiff price</u>.
一項新的研究指出，針對富人增稅的國家可能會付出高昂的代價。

實用短語 / 用法 / 句型

1. (as) stiff as a board 非常僵硬的

The man's body was <u>as stiff as a board</u> when it was found in the snow.

這名男子在雪地裡被發現時，他的身體已經僵硬。

2. stiff and formal 生硬、不自然的

You had better revise your manuscript. The words tend to sound <u>stiff and formal</u>.

你最好修改一下草稿，你的用字聽起來很生硬。

Straight

直的、正的；坦誠的、直率的；嚴肅的；僅涉及兩者的；整齊的；連續不間斷的；互不欠錢的

▶ MP3-139

straight answer　直接了當的答案

I just want a <u>straight answer</u> to the question.
我只是想要這個問題的明確答案。

straight arrow　正直坦率的人

Friends describe him as a <u>straight arrow</u> who rarely drinks and cares much about his family.
朋友都說他是個正直坦率的人，不太喝酒而且非常關心家人。

straight shooter　說話坦誠直接的人

Being a <u>straight shooter</u> sometimes gets me into trouble.
說話太直接有時候讓我陷入麻煩。

straight talk / talking　實話實說、有話直說

Most people like <u>straight talk</u> and hate hypocrites.
大多數人喜歡有話直說，不喜歡偽君子。

straight face　一臉正經的表情、繃著臉

He looked ridiculous in leather trousers, and I was desperately trying to keep a <u>straight face</u>.
他穿皮褲的樣子很好笑，但我還是拼了命裝作一臉正經。

straight choice 僅有兩種可能的選擇

It is a <u>straight choice</u> between my career or my family.
我只有兩種選擇，要不事業，要不就家庭。

straight exchange / swap 兩者直接的交換

Let's do a <u>straight swap</u>—your guitar for my skateboard.
做個爽快的交換吧！你用吉他和我換滑板！

1. to be straight

如果兩人「are straight」，指他們互不欠錢的、扯平的
（口語用法，不用於名詞前）

You bought the movie tickets, so if I pay for the dinner, we'll be straight.
你買了電影票，所以如果我付晚餐錢，那麼我們就扯平了。

2. to be straight with sb 對某人坦誠

If you had been straight with us, none of this mess would have happened.
如果你當初對我們說實話，就不會有現在混亂的局面。

3. to get / put sth straight 把某物整理好

It only took us an hour to get the flat straight after the party.
派對後，我們只花了 1 個小時就把公寓整理好了。

4. to get / set sth straight 把某事弄清楚

Let me get this straight—Adam sold the car and gave you the money?
讓我把這事搞清楚，你說亞當把車賣了然後把錢給你？

5. to put / set sb straight (+ on sth)

確保某人了解真相

Don't worry. I will set her straight on this matter.
不用擔心，我會把這件事跟她說清楚的。

6. to put / set the record straight 澄清事實

He's decided to write his memoirs to <u>set the record straight</u> once and for all.
他決定寫回憶錄來徹底澄清事實。

7. (as) straight as a die 筆直的；完全坦白的、誠實的

The road runs <u>straight as a die</u> for 50 or so miles.
這條路筆直延伸了 50 英里左右。

He's <u>as straight as a die</u>. I can trust him to tell me what he's really thinking.
他非常坦白，我相信他會告訴我真實的想法。

8. straight + days / games / wins

指連續的一段時間或是連續的勝利

They're the only team to have won <u>seventy-three straight games</u> this season.
他們是本季唯一一支獲得 73 連勝的隊伍。

Striking 顯著的、驚人的、出眾的、引人注目的

striking aspect 突出的、引人注意的方面

From the outside, the most <u>striking aspect</u> of the building is its tall tower.
從外觀來看，這棟建築物最突出的地方就是它的高塔。

striking contrast / difference 鮮明的對比 / 很大的不同

There's a <u>striking contrast</u> between what he does and what he says he does.
他說的和他做的大相逕庭。

striking example / illustration 顯著的例子

The library is a <u>striking example</u> of Baroque architecture.
這間圖書館是巴洛克式建築的經典範例。

She offered a <u>striking illustration</u> of the point that I was making.
針對我的論點，她提出了一個很好的例子。

striking feature 顯著的特色

The most <u>striking feature</u> of those statistics is the high proportion of suicides.
這些統計數據最驚人的點在於高自殺率。

striking finding / result 驚人的發現、結果

One of the most <u>striking findings</u> was that excessive speed contributes to serious and fatal accidents.
最驚人的發現是，超速會造成嚴重及致命的意外。

striking illustration / image / picture / portrait
吸引人的圖像、照片

Her collection includes <u>striking images</u> of the city in the snow.
她的收藏包含這個城市的驚人雪景。

striking landscape / view 驚人的、吸引人的景象

The cave frames a <u>striking view</u> across the bay.
這個洞穴在海灣上形成一個驚人的美景。

striking likeness / parallel / resemblance / similarity
驚人的相似、極度相似

The book bears several <u>striking similarities</u> to last year's bestseller.
這個作品和去年的暢銷書有幾處極度相似。

striking look 出眾的外表

Emma Watson is known for her <u>striking</u> good <u>looks</u> and her sharp mind.
艾瑪華森以她出眾的外表和敏銳的思維出名。

Strong 強壯的；堅定的；強烈的；有力的；穩固的、（關係）緊密的；很有可能的；（味道、氣味）濃的；擅長的

strong constitution 強健的體格

This young man is blessed with a strong constitution.
這個年輕人有強健的體格。

strong point / suit 優點、強項

Patience is not my strong suit.
我沒什麼耐性。

strong belief / conviction 堅定的信念

We have a strong conviction that we can hardly make any money in the stock market.
我們很堅信我們在股票市場中賺不了什麼錢。

strong commitment
堅定的承諾；強烈的責任感；強烈的堅持

He has a strong commitment to the quality of teaching.
他對教學品質有強烈的堅持。

strong desire 強烈的慾望

The man has a strong desire for personal independence and privacy.
這個人強烈要求個人的獨立與隱私。

strong emphasis / focus 非常強調、強烈關注

Our company places a particularly <u>strong emphasis</u> on customer care.
我們公司特別注重顧客服務。

strong idea / opinion / view 固執的意見、強烈的觀點

He has <u>strong views</u> on some of the pervading issues in the current education system.
他對現行教育體制普遍存在的一些問題有強烈的看法。

strong impression 深刻的印象

His failure to keep to his pledge gave a <u>strong impression</u> of poor faith.
他食言一事，讓人對他的不守信用印象深刻。

strong influence 強烈的影響

Such news may have a <u>strong influence</u> over your opinions on this presidential candidate.
這樣的新聞可能會強烈影響你對這位總統候選人的看法。

strong language 冒犯的、強烈的言辭

The film contains <u>strong language</u> and violence, which are not appropriate for children.
電影內容涉及不雅言語和大量暴力，不宜兒童觀賞。

strong nerves

很大的膽量、強大的心理素質（也可以説 strong stomach）

You need <u>strong nerves</u> to work in an emergency room.
在急診室工作需要有強大的心理素質。

strong opposition 強烈反對

Her decision to marry the man met with <u>strong opposition</u> from family and friends.
她打算嫁給這個男人的決定受到家人和朋友的強烈反對。

strong sense of sth 強烈的～感

He has a <u>strong sense of</u> responsibility to his vocation of teaching.
他對自己的教學工作富有強烈的責任感。

strong support 強烈、大力支持

The policy implemented last month received <u>strong support</u> from parents.
上個月開始施行的政策獲得家長的大力支持。

strong temptation 強烈的誘惑

There's always a <u>strong temptation</u> to put off doing assignments and hang out with friends first.
總有先和朋友出去，作業晚點再做的強烈誘惑。

strong will 強大的、堅定的意志

She has proven to be skillful and seems to have a very strong will.
事實證明了她技術高超且似乎有著強大的意志力。

strong argument / case 有力的論據、理由

The testimony offered a strong case for acquitting her on grounds of self-defense.
這證詞替無罪釋放她提供充分有力的理由，因為她的行為是出於自我防衛。

strong currency / market 強勢貨幣 / 行情看好的市場

Compared with the New Taiwan dollar, the US dollar is a strong currency.
相較於台幣，美元是強勢貨幣。

strong evidence 有力的證據

The figures provide strong evidence of his being a suitable candidate for this position.
數據提供有力的證據證明他能勝任這個職位。

strong leadership 強而有力的領導

Being a good boss needs strong leadership.
要成為一個好老闆需要有強大的領導能力。

strong base / foundation 穩固的基礎

This agreement laid a <u>strong foundation</u> for future cooperation between the two countries.
這協議替未來兩國合作奠定穩固的基礎。

strong connection / link 緊密的連結

We have <u>strong connections</u> with other departments working in the same area.
我們和同在這裡的其他部門有緊密的連結。

strong relationship 緊密的關係

We look forward to establishing a <u>strong</u> working <u>relationship</u> with your team.
我們期待和貴團隊建立緊密的合作關係。

strong candidate 有機會的、有可能的人選

The interviewer said I was a <u>strong candidate</u> because of my previous experience in marketing.
面試官說因為我有市場行銷的經驗，因此我是可能的人選。

strong chance / possibility / probability 很大的可能

There is a <u>strong possibility</u> of another Korean war, with potentially devastating consequences.
很有可能會發生另一個韓戰，還可能帶來毀滅性的後果。

strong coffee / drink / tea 濃咖啡 / 烈酒 / 濃茶

I kept away from <u>strong coffee</u> for years, but recently I've begun to backslide.
我好幾年不喝濃的咖啡，但最近我又禁不住誘惑了。

strong flavor / smell / taste 濃烈的味道 / 氣味

Not everyone loves the <u>strong flavor</u> of blue cheese.
並不是每個人都喜歡藍乳酪那濃烈的味道。

實用短語 / 用法 / 句型　　▶ MP3-143

1. **to be in / gain a strong position**
   佔有強勢的、主宰的地位
   The company <u>is in a strong position</u> in the shoe industry.
   這間公司在鞋業佔有強勢的地位。

2. **to be strong on sth** 擅長某事
   The boy <u>is not strong on</u> interacting with people.
   這男孩不擅長和人互動。

3. **(as) strong as a(n) horse / ox** 強壯如牛
   The athletes on our team are all <u>as strong as a horse</u>.
   我們隊上的運動員都壯得像牛一樣。

Superficial 外表的、表面上的；粗淺的、草率的；膚淺的

▶ MP3-144

superficial damage / injury 表面的受損 / 皮肉傷

Fortunately, the storm caused only <u>superficial damage</u> to the building.
所幸這場暴風雨只對建築物的表面造成損壞。

superficial level 表面上

At a <u>superficial level</u>, things seem to have remained the same.
表面上看來，事情似乎沒有變化。

superficial resemblance / similarity 表面上的相似

In spite of their <u>superficial similarities</u>, the two games are, in fact, fundamentally different.
儘管表面上有些相似，但實際上這兩款遊戲非常不同。

superficial knowledge / understanding
粗淺的了解、認識

Before reading this book, I only had a <u>superficial knowledge</u> of the man's life and career.
在讀這本書之前，我對這個人的一生和事業只有粗淺的了解。

Swift 快速的、立即的

▶ MP3-145

swift action 立即的行動

The police took swift action against the mob.
警方採取立即行動對付幫派份子。

swift decision 快速的決定

We have to take swift decisions when situations are tense and demanding.
當情勢緊急嚴峻時，我們必須快速做出決定。

swift reply / response 立即的回覆

Thank you for your swift reply.
感謝您的即時回覆。

Tall 高的；誇大的

▶ MP3-146

tall order 難以做到的事情

Building the bridge in time for the Olympics will be a <u>tall order</u>.
要趕在奧運前蓋好這座橋是很難的事。

tall story / tale 誇大的事、難以置信的事

I can't find any information. Is this just a <u>tall tale</u> or is it true?
我找不到任何的資訊，這只是誇大還是真的？

實用短語 / 用法 / 句型 ▶ MP3-147

1. **to stand / walk tall** 昂首闊步、滿懷自信
   As he walked up to the podium to speak, he reminded himself to <u>stand tall</u>.
   當他走上台演講時，他提醒自己要有自信。

Tentative 暫定的、試驗性的、試探性的

▶ MP3-148

tentative agreement 暫時的、初步的協議

Workers have reached a <u>tentative agreement</u> with management.
工人和管理階層已經達成初步協議。

tentative conclusion 暫定的、初步的結論

The official stressed that the report was based on <u>tentative conclusions</u> and said the analysis was not yet final.
這位官員強調，這份報告是基於初步的結論，並表示分析還未完成。

tentative plan / proposal 暫定的計畫 / 提議

The two organizations are already drawing up <u>tentative plans</u> and discussing a joint approach to developing a national stadium.
這兩個組織已經在擬定初步的計畫，並討論興建國家體育館的共同方法。

tentative step 試驗性的措施；試探性的步伐

The government is taking <u>tentative steps</u> towards tackling the country's economic problems.
政府正採取試驗性的措施來解決國家的經濟問題。

Thin

瘦的；細的、薄的；稀少的、稀薄的；空泛的、微弱的

▶ MP3-149

thin skin 臉皮薄

She has such <u>thin skin</u> that she can't even take a little good-natured teasing.
她的臉皮這麼薄，連一點無傷大雅的玩笑都開不起。

thin market 交易冷清的市場

It takes years for a new ship to be designed and built, and investment in such a <u>thin market</u> can appear risky.
一艘新船從設計到生產需要好幾年的時間，投資這樣冷門的市場有風險。

thin air 稀薄的空氣

Because of the <u>thin air</u> and high altitude along with the ice and snow on the surface, this has become the coldest place in the world.
稀薄的空氣和高海拔，再加上地表的冰雪，讓這裡成為世界上最冷的地方。

thin argument / evidence / excuse
薄弱的論點 / 證據 / 藉口

Even if the optimists' theory is true, it still seems a <u>thin argument</u> against the reform.
就算樂觀主義者的理論沒錯，這個反對改革的論點仍然薄弱。

thin plot 空洞的劇情

In spite of the <u>thin plot</u>, the acting in the movie is marvelous.
儘管劇情空洞，這部電影演員的演技仍然一流。

thin smile 淺淺的微笑

He gave a <u>thin smile</u> that conveyed little more than feigned interest.
他淺淺的微笑表示，他對此沒有太大興趣。

thin voice 微弱的聲音

When he was settling down for a nap, he heard a <u>thin voice</u> from the outside.
就在他準備坐下來小睡一下時，他聽見外面傳來微弱的聲音。

實用短語 / 用法 / 句型　　▶ MP3-150

1. **to be thin on the ground** （可用的）寥寥無幾
   Taxis <u>are thin on the ground</u> now, so I am afraid that we have to go home on foot.
   現在計程車寥寥無幾，我看我們可能要走路回家了。

2. **to disappear / vanish into thin air** 消失得無影無蹤
   Where could the escaped prisoners go? They can't just <u>disappear into thin air</u>.
   逃犯可以去哪？他們不可能就這樣憑空消失。

A
B
C
D
E
F
G
H
I
J
K
L
M
N
O
P
Q
R
S
T
U

3. to have a thin time (of it)

日子不太好過、有不愉快的經驗

He lost his job last year and his family has been <u>having a thin time of it</u>.

他去年丟了工作，現在家人的生活都不太好過。

4. to walk / skate / tread on thin ice

如履薄冰、情況危急

I try to stay focused so I don't end up <u>skating on thin ice</u> when the teacher asks me a question.

我試著保持專注，這樣一來，老師問我問題時，才不至於戰戰兢兢。

5. to wear thin 漸漸失去耐心；（因出現太多而）失去吸引力、不再有效

I have warned him several times about being late and my patience is <u>wearing thin</u>.

我多次警告他不要遲到，我對他已經失去耐心了。

His standard excuse for being late was beginning to <u>wear thin</u>.

他遲到常用的藉口已經開始不管用了。

6. (as) thin as a rail / rake 骨瘦如柴

She eats like a horse and yet she's still <u>as thin as a rake</u>.

她吃很多卻還是骨瘦如柴。

7. out of thin air 突然冒出來、不知道從哪來的

The magician just produced coins <u>out of thin air</u>.

魔術師憑空變出了幾枚硬幣。

8. **paper-thin / wafer-thin** 極薄

The rooms were divided only by a <u>wafer-thin</u> partition wall.
房間只用極薄的隔板隔開。

9. **razor-thin margin / victory**
極小的差距 / 微幅領先的勝利

The president won the election by a <u>razor-thin margin</u>.
這位總統以極小的差距贏得大選。

10. the thin end of the wedge 冰山一角

Employees believe the job cuts are just <u>the thin end of the wedge</u>.
員工認為裁員只是冰山一角罷了。

11. thin on top 頭髮稀疏

I noticed that the teacher was getting <u>thin on top</u>.
我發現這老師的頭頂越來越禿了。

12. through thick and thin 患難與共

Kevin is someone I can trust because we have gone <u>through thick and thin,</u> through good times and bad times.
凱文是我可以信賴的人，因為我們曾經患難與共。

Tight 嚴格的；緊的、緊密的；勢均力敵的

▶ MP3-151

tight constraint / control / regulation / restriction
嚴格的控制、限制

The government exercises <u>tight control</u> over media coverage.
政府對媒體報導進行嚴格管控。

Despite <u>tight restrictions</u> and <u>regulations</u>, the number of civil society organizations has continued to grow.
儘管限制和規定嚴格，公民社會組織的數量仍持續增長。

tight security 嚴格的防衛措施、戒備森嚴

The jewels have been kept at a secret location under <u>tight security</u>.
珠寶被存放在戒備森嚴的祕密地點。

tight budget 有限的預算

He started his business on a <u>tight budget</u> and could not afford to overspend.
他用有限的預算創業，不能有任何超支。

tight bend / corner 急轉彎

They collided on a <u>tight bend</u> and both cars were seriously damaged.
他們在急轉彎處相撞，兩車都嚴重損壞。

tight deadline 緊迫的期限

The ability to cope with tight deadlines is essential.
處理緊迫期限的能力相當重要。

tight margin 有限的利潤

The company is operating at very tight margins.
這間公司的營業利潤非常低。

tight muscle 緊繃的肌肉

It's better to do some warm-ups and stretch your tight muscles before the contest.
比賽前最好先暖身、伸展緊繃的肌肉。

tight schedule 緊湊的行程

It's difficult to cram anything into the tight schedule.
這個緊湊的行程很難再塞進任何東西了。

tight contest / game / match / race 勢均力敵的比賽

We think that it will be a tight contest and the first goal could be crucial.
我們覺得這會是一場勢均力敵的球賽，而且第 1 分可能至關重要。

1. to keep a tight grip / hold / rein on sth
對～嚴加控制

What the company has to do is to <u>keep a tight rein on</u> its spending until the financial situation improves.
公司現在該做的是，對支出嚴加管控直到財務狀況好轉。

2. to run a tight ship 嚴格管理（公司、組織）

They have been <u>running a tight ship</u> for many years in terms of financial control.
他們已經嚴格控管公司的財務許多年了。

3. to sleep tight 睡個好覺、一夜好眠

Did you <u>sleep tight</u> last night?
你昨晚睡得好嗎？

4. in a tight corner / spot 陷入困境

Employers may find themselves <u>in a tight corner</u> if they attempt to increase employee benefits or increase profits.
雇主在試圖增加員工福利或提高盈餘時，可能會陷入兩難。

5. money is tight 手頭很緊

My <u>money is tight</u> and I need a job badly.
我的手頭很緊，非常需要一份工作。

6. time is tight 時間緊湊

Her <u>time is tight</u>, and she has another meeting to go to this afternoon.

她的時間緊湊，下午還有一場會要開。

Tough （肉）過熟的、咬不動的；難對付的、強硬的；堅強的、堅定的；艱難的 ▶ MP3-153

tough meat　咬不動的肉

The <u>meat</u> was really <u>tough</u> and hard to chew.
這塊肉太熟了，咬不動。

tough battle / match　艱辛的比賽、苦戰

I think it was a mentally <u>tough battle</u> today, especially in the five sets against Federer.
我認為今天的比賽是一場精神上的苦戰，尤其是對上費德勒的那 5 盤。

tough cookie　難纏、難相處的人；堅定不放棄的人

There was a <u>tough cookie</u> that demanded to see the manager in here this morning.
早上有一位難纏的客人要求要見經理。

He had a difficult childhood, but he's a <u>tough cookie</u>. I know he'll be a success one day.
他童年過得很辛苦，但他很堅強，我相信有一天他會成功的。

tough critic　刻薄、嚴苛的評論者

He is known as a <u>tough critic</u> when it comes to food.
在吃的方面，他是嚴苛的美食評論家。

tough customer 難應付的顧客

Brian is a <u>tough customer</u>. Just keep away from him.
布萊恩是很難應付的客人，離他遠一點。

tough nut (to crack)

棘手的問題；難應付的人（也可以說 hard nut to crack）

Overcoming local trade barriers is going to be a <u>tough nut to crack</u>.
克服當地的貿易壁壘將會是個棘手的難題。

tough line 強硬的立場

We are prepared to take a <u>tough line</u> in negotiating with the company.
和公司談判時，我們打算採取強硬的立場。

tough problem / question 棘手的問題

The reporters fired <u>tough questions</u> at the spokesperson from all angles.
記者從各個面向對發言人提出棘手的問題。

tough call / decision 艱難的決定

When making a <u>tough decision</u>, you should always think twice before you leap.
在做艱難決定時，你一定要三思而後行。

tough luck 真倒楣（表示同情）

I'm sorry to hear about your accident. <u>Tough luck</u>.
聽到你的意外我很遺憾，只能説你運氣不好。

tough sell 很難讓人接受的事物（也可以説 hard sell）

A tax increase is always a <u>tough sell</u> to voters.
增税一直都是選民很難接受的事。

tough time 艱困的日子、時期

The company is going through a <u>tough time</u> at the moment.
這家公司正經歷一段艱困的時期。

實用短語 / 用法 / 句型　　▶ MP3-154

1. **to be / get tough on sb** 對某人而言很艱困的
   Having to stay indoors all day <u>is tough on</u> a kid.
   對小孩來説，要整天待在家裡很困難。

2. **(as) tough as nails / old boots**
   非常硬的、咬不動的；堅強的、堅韌不屈的
   It turns out that my granddad is <u>as tough as nails</u>
   and will never give in.
   我發現爺爺非常堅強、從不願意放棄。

Toxic

有毒的；令人極不愉快的、惡毒的、造成陰影的

toxic chemicals / fumes / gas / smoke / substance / waste 有毒化學物 / 煙霧 / 氣體 / 煙霧 / 物質 / 廢料

The photographer disclosed that the factory directly discharged toxic waste into the river.
攝影師發現這間工廠直接將有毒廢料排進河流中。

toxic effect / reaction 毒性作用、有毒反應

This new treatment can reduce the toxic effect that many current cancer therapies have on healthy cells.
這個新療法可以減少目前許多癌症療法對健康細胞造成的毒性作用。

toxic atmosphere 險惡的、令人不愉快的氛圍

His attitude added poison to an already toxic atmosphere, making compromise far more unlikely.
他的態度使原本就很不愉快的氛圍雪上加霜，也使協商越來越不可能。

toxic parent 惡毒的父母

The novel depicts a five-year-old girl held captive in a small room by her toxic parents.
這本小說描述一位 5 歲的小女孩被惡毒的父母親囚禁在小房間裡。

toxic relationship 讓人產生陰影的關係

She is clearly in a <u>toxic relationship</u> and she needs to get out of it.

她顯然處於一種不良的關係中，她必須擺脫這段關係。

Vague 模糊的、不清楚的

▶ MP3-156

vague description / promise / statement / term

含糊的描述 / 承諾 / 發言 / 措辭

Candidates under election pressure tend to make <u>vague promises</u> of reform.
在選戰壓力下，候選人往往會對改革做出模糊的承諾。

vague feeling / sense 隱約的感覺

He had a <u>vague feeling</u> that something was wrong.
他隱約覺得事情不太對勁。

vague idea / notion 不太了解、模糊的想法

Many college students have only a <u>vague idea</u> of what they want to do after they graduate.
很多大學生在畢業之後不清楚自己想做什麼。

vague impression 模糊的印象

Everything happens so quickly that all we are left with is a <u>vague impression</u>.
一切都發生得太快，我們留下的只有一個模糊的印象。

vague memory / recollection 模糊的記憶

The man had only a <u>vague memory</u> of what happened last night.
男子不太記得昨晚發生了什麼事。

vague outline / shape 模糊的輪廓

We could just barely see the <u>vague outline</u> of the plane in the sky.
我們只能勉強看到飛機在空中模糊的輪廓。

Vigorous

激烈的、強烈的；有力的、積極的；旺盛的、茁壯的

▶ MP3-157

vigorous activity / exercise 劇烈的運動

As little as 30-minute <u>vigorous exercise</u> once a week will significantly reduce the risk of cardiovascular diseases.
每週只要做一次 30 分鐘的劇烈運動，就能大幅降低心血管疾病的風險。

vigorous debate / defense / discussion

激烈的辯論 / 辯護 / 討論

There was <u>vigorous debate</u> on the question of whether our party should stand for election.
關於我們黨是否應該參選的問題有激烈的辯論。

vigorous opposition / protest 強烈的反對 / 抗議

There has been <u>vigorous opposition</u> to the proposal for a pipeline in that area.
在該地埋輸油管的計畫遭到強烈反對。

vigorous action / campaign / program

有力的、激烈的行動 / 運動 / 計畫

A <u>vigorous campaign</u> to save the historic site attracted overwhelming support.
拯救古蹟的激烈社運獲得了廣泛支持。

vigorous effort / pursuit 積極努力 / 追求

Since the war, <u>vigorous efforts</u> have been made to rebuild the economy.
戰後要重建經濟需要積極的努力。

vigorous growth 蓬勃發展、成長旺盛

It is expected that this campaign will lead to <u>vigorous growth</u> of the number of customers.
預計這次的活動能大幅提升來客數。

Weak

弱的；無力的；無能的、沒影響力的；疲軟的、蕭條的；稀的、淡的

weak heart / lungs / stomach

心臟不太好 / 肺不太好 / 胃不太好

Her grandmother suffered from a <u>weak heart</u>.
她奶奶心臟不太好。

weak smile 勉強一笑

In spite of my disappointment, I managed to offer a <u>weak smile</u>.
儘管失望，我還是勉強擠出笑容。

weak argument / case / excuse 站不住腳的論據、理由

What you just said is a relatively <u>weak argument</u>.
你剛剛的說法相對站不住腳。

weak currency 弱勢貨幣

A <u>weaker</u> domestic <u>currency</u> will be good news for a country's exporters.
較弱勢的國內貨幣對一個國家的出口商來說會是一大福音。

weak evidence 無力的、站不住腳的證據

The <u>evidence</u> in support of this idea seems <u>weak</u> and insufficient.
支持這個想法的證據不夠而且站不住腳。

weak government 無能的政府

The columnist blamed the <u>weak government</u> for the current financial crisis.
專欄作家指責無能政府是造成當前金融危機的罪魁禍首。

weak leadership 軟弱的領導能力

The opposition party has been urging the prime minister to resign, accusing him of <u>weak leadership</u>.
反對黨勸首相下台，指責他沒有領導能力。

weak link 薄弱的環節

They are a fairly good team; the only <u>weak link</u> is the relatively inexperienced goalkeeper.
他們是一支很棒的球隊，唯一薄弱的環節是其經驗相對不足的守門員。

weak point / spot 弱點、弱項

Targeting the opponent's <u>weak spots</u> is a typical technique in debates.
針對對手的弱點攻擊是辯論的典型策略。

weak position 劣勢、不利的狀態

If you do not have alternatives, you are in a <u>weak position</u>.
如果沒有替代方案，你就處於劣勢。

weak economy / industry 蕭條的經濟 / 產業

When the <u>economy</u> is <u>weak</u>, it is very hard for suppliers to raise their prices.
經濟不景氣時，供應商很難提高價格。

weak coffee / drink / tea 淡咖啡 / 薄酒 / 清茶

I am very sensitive to caffeine. I cannot even stand <u>weak tea</u>.
我對咖啡因很敏感，連清茶都不能喝。

實用短語 / 用法 / 句型

▶ MP3-159

1. **to be weak in / on sth** 不擅長某事
   The stereotype still exists that boys <u>are weak in</u> languages but strong in science.
   男生科學較強、語言較弱的刻板印象仍然存在。

2. **a weak moment** 心軟的、容易被說服的時候
   In <u>a weak moment</u>, I agreed to lend him 50,000 dollars.
   我一時心軟答應要借他 5 萬元。

3. **weak at the knees**
   （因為看到或談到非常喜歡的人，或讓人害怕的事而）膝蓋發軟的、雙腿發軟的
   The thought of seeing him made me go <u>weak at the knees</u>.
   一想到會看到他就讓我膝蓋發軟。

Wide 寬的；很大的；廣泛的

▶ MP3-160

wide circulation 發行量很大

This book enjoys a <u>wide circulation</u> of more than three thousand within a month.
這本書的發行量在一個月內就超過 3 千冊。

wide difference / diversity / variation
很大的不同、變化

There is <u>wide variation</u> in sizes, methods of construction, and design.
在尺寸、做法和設計上都有很大的不同。

wide gap / margin 很大的差距

There is a <u>wide gap</u> between the rich and the poor in our country.
我們國家的貧富差距很大。

wide agreement 廣泛的共識

There is <u>wide agreement</u> among the general public that atmospheric pollution is the result of industrialization.
民眾一致認為空氣污染是工業化的後果。

wide array / choice / selection 廣泛的選項、大量

We visited the local market and saw a <u>wide array</u> of fruit and vegetables.
我們去了當地市場，看到各式各樣的蔬果。

wide assortment / variety 廣泛的種類

You can find a <u>wide variety</u> of courses on this website.
你可以在這個網站上找到各種課程。

wide experience 豐富的經驗

This position calls for somebody with <u>wide</u> work <u>experience</u> in banking.
這個職位需要豐富的銀行工作經驗。

wide publicity 廣泛的關注、宣傳

The department store's opening ceremony successfully attracted <u>wide publicity</u>.
這間百貨公司的開幕活動成功吸引了大眾關注。

wide range / scope / spectrum 廣泛的範圍

A <u>wide range</u> of singers and artists will perform in this year's countdown party.
許多歌手和藝人將在今年的跨年晚會上表演。

wider audience / public 更廣泛的群眾

These issues may be of interest to a <u>wider audience</u>.
更多的人可能會對這些議題感興趣。

wider debate / issue 更廣泛的爭論 / 問題

The problem raises <u>wider issues</u> of gender and identity.
這個問題引起更廣泛的性別及身分認同議題。

wide support 廣泛的支持

The idea, being too conservative, no longer enjoys <u>wide support</u>.
這個太過保守的想法不再受到廣泛的支持。

實用短語 / 用法 / 句型　　▶ MP3-161

1. **to be wide of the mark** 錯誤的、不準確的、不是所需要的

   Sandy failed the course because everything she did <u>was wide of the mark</u>.
   珊迪這門課被當，因為她所做的都不是課程需要的。

2. **to give a wide berth** 和～保持距離

   The doctor advised him to <u>give a wide berth</u> to cigarettes after his illness.
   在他生病之後，醫生建議他要戒菸。

3. **far and wide** 到處

The police searched <u>far and wide</u> for the missing girl.

警察到處搜尋失蹤的小女孩。

4. **wide awake** 完全清醒的

She could not relax and still felt <u>wide awake</u> after lying down for an hour.

她躺了 1 個小時仍然無法放鬆，還是非常清醒。

Widespread 普遍的、廣泛的 ▶ MP3-162

widespread abuse / adoption / deployment / practice / usage / use 廣泛使用、運用

The widespread use of pesticides upsets the natural balance.
農藥的廣泛使用打亂了自然生態平衡。

widespread acceptance / agreement / popularity / recognition / support 普遍接受、支持

Alternative medicines are now winning widespread acceptance among doctors.
替代性藥物現在被醫生普遍接受。

widespread acclaim / praise 廣泛的讚許

His achievements have earned him widespread academic acclaim.
他的成就贏得了學術界廣泛的讚譽。

widespread anger / condemnation / criticism 廣泛的憤怒 / 譴責 / 批評

The design for the new mascot has attracted widespread criticism.
新吉祥物的設計引起廣泛的批評。

widespread assumption / speculation

普遍的假設 / 猜測

Psychological research has overturned this <u>widespread assumption</u> and belief.
心理學的研究已經推翻了這個普遍的假設和想法。

widespread belief / feeling / perception 普遍的想法

There is a <u>widespread perception</u> that the corporation is now in financial trouble.
很多人認為這家企業陷入財務困境。

widespread concern / fear / panic 普遍擔心 / 害怕

There is <u>widespread concern</u> that such intense tourism might do harm to marine ecology.
民眾普遍擔心，如此蓬勃的旅遊業可能會破壞海洋生態。

widespread confusion 普遍困惑

There is <u>widespread confusion</u> among the public about the education reform.
民眾普遍對這個教育改革感到困惑。

widespread consensus 普遍的共識

There is, in fact, <u>widespread consensus</u> among economists about what steps should be taken next.
事實上，經濟學家已經對下一步取得普遍的共識。

widespread corruption / disease / poverty / unemployment 普遍的貪污 / 疾病 / 貧窮 / 失業

Thanks to the report, systematic oppression and <u>widespread corruption</u> were brought to light.
由於媒體的報導，體制壓迫和普遍的貪污問題被爆了出來。

widespread coverage / dissemination / distribution / publicity 廣泛報導、宣傳

There has been <u>widespread coverage</u> in many national newspapers about the scandal.
這則醜聞在許多全國性的報紙上都有大幅報導。

widespread damage / destruction / devastation 廣泛破壞

The <u>widespread destruction</u> of woodland has made life harder for many animals.
森林的大面積破壞使許多動物的生活更加艱難。

widespread discontent / dissatisfaction 普遍的不滿

The survey found customers' <u>widespread dissatisfaction</u> with the company's customer service.
這項調查發現，消費者普遍對公司的售後服務感到不滿。

widespread interest 廣泛的興趣、關注

A global competition to name the new seven wonders of the world has attracted <u>widespread interest</u>.
全球評選世界新 7 大奇景的活動受到民眾廣泛關注。

widespread opposition 普遍反對

There is no slight decline in animal testing globally despite <u>widespread opposition</u>.
儘管受到普遍反對，全球動物實驗的數量卻絲毫沒有減少。

memo

memo

memo

memo

國家圖書館出版品預行編目資料
....
搭配詞的力量Collocations：形容詞篇 / 王梓沅著
-- 初版 -- 臺北市：瑞蘭國際, 2018.07
304面；14.8×21公分 -- （外語達人系列；19）
ISBN：978-986-96580-4-1（平裝附光碟片）
1.英語 2.形容詞
....
805.164   107009909

外語達人系列 19

搭配詞的力量 _{形容詞篇}
Collocations

作者｜王梓沅・作者助理｜胡嘉修・責任編輯｜林珊玉、王愿琦
校對｜王梓沅、胡嘉修、林珊玉、王愿琦

封面設計｜蔡嘉恩・版型設計、內文排版｜陳如琪

瑞蘭國際出版

董事長｜張暖彗・社長兼總編輯｜王愿琦
編輯部
副總編輯｜葉仲芸・副主編｜潘治婷・文字編輯｜林珊玉、鄧元婷・特約文字編輯｜楊嘉怡
設計部主任｜余佳憓・美術編輯｜陳如琪
業務部
副理｜楊米琪・組長｜林湲洵・專員｜張毓庭

出版社｜瑞蘭國際有限公司・地址｜台北市大安區安和路一段104號7樓之1
電話｜(02)2700-4625・傳真｜(02)2700-4622・訂購專線｜(02)2700-4625
劃撥帳號｜19914152 瑞蘭國際有限公司・瑞蘭國際網路書城｜www.genki-japan.com.tw

法律顧問｜海灣國際法律事務所　呂錦峯律師

總經銷｜聯合發行股份有限公司・電話｜(02)2917-8022、2917-8042
傳真｜(02)2915-6275、2915-7212・印刷｜科億印刷股份有限公司
出版日期｜2018年07月初版1刷・定價｜420元・ISBN｜978-986-96580-4-1
　　　　　2019年05月初版2刷